THE LEBENSBORN EXPERIMENT

BOOK 1

THE LEBENSBORN EXPERIMENT

BOOK 1

by

JOYCE YVETTE DAVIS

CITIOFBOOKS, INC.
3736 Eubank NE Suite A1
Albuquerque, NM 87111-3579
www.citiofbooks.com

Hotline: 1 (877) 389-2759
Fax: 1 (505) 930-7244

Ordering Information:
Quantity sales. Special discounts are available on quantity purchases by corporations, associations, and others. For details, contact the publisher at the address above.

Printed in the United States of America.

| ISBN-13: | Paperback | 979-8-89391-308-8 |
| | eBook | 979-8-89391-309-5 |

Library of Congress Control Number: 2024919062

In Loving Memory of my Father,
George Henry Davis,
and my Brother,
Gerald Paxton Davis

FORWARD

In his address to German Officers on September 7, 1940, Heinrich Himmler, Minister of Interior and head of the Gestapo, stated: "In the eleven years during which I have been Reichfuhrer SS, my aim has always been the same: to create an Order of good blood that can serve Germany and commit itself without sparing itself; to create an Order that will so spread the idea of Nordic blood that we shall attract to us all the Nordic blood in the world; to deprive our enemies of that blood and annex it to ourselves. We must take it for ourselves, and the others must have none."

To facilitate the Reich's plan of "annexing all people of Nordic blood to Germany," the welfare organization known as the Lebensborn Register Society (Fountain of Life) was used to house children stolen from other countries who were to be adopted by German parents. The Lebensborn Society existed long before the war and was first established as maternity homes to care for both married and unwed mothers and their children.

All over Europe, thousands of "racially valuable" children from six months to twelve years old were taken from their families to be "Germanized."

Records of the Nuremberg Trials indicated that there were over 200,000 Polish children kidnapped, and more than 50,000 children abducted from Ruthenia. Children whose appearance didn't meet the Nordic ideal, i.e., blonde hair and blue eyes, or whose ethnic origin was questionable, were taken to concentration camps. Only a few abducted children returned home to their parents.

The kidnapped children were brainwashed and told their parents no longer wanted them. Some children were sold or given away, and many mistreated.

Others were used in experiments to endow them with physical attributes that would further the claim of Nordic superiority and satisfy the Reich's relentless obsession to create a master race of Aryan Super Humans. This story is of one of those children and the unexpected results that followed.

CHAPTER ONE

"What a chimera then is man?
what a strange creature,
what a monster, what chaos,
what a combination of contradictions,
what a prodigy!
Judge of all matters, imbecile worm of the earth,
Depository of truth;
Gutter of incertitude and glory and disgrace of
the universe."

Unknown Author

Germany, April 28, 1945

It wouldn't be long now before the boy was dead.

In agony, the boy screamed and screamed until his throat was raw and bleeding until his screams no longer sounded like that of a ten-year-old child but the squealing of a small wounded animal caught in the snare of a hunter's trap. The snare was the cold steel of an operating table where his ghostly white, naked flesh lay bound.

Somewhere in the Black Forest of Germany, high in a dingy tower of a medieval castle, his captors anxiously awaited his death. The hunters were members of the boy's own race, prowling the earth like a pack of ravenous Pit Bulls while raging war with the rest of the human race for total domination of the world.

Death for the boy stretched on for hours until finally, it took him at midnight.

Hovering over the dead boy's body were two Pit Bulls of notorious distinction. The younger was a member of the SS and one of the many leaders of the pack, an Oberstfuhrer named Otto Strauss. He was exceptionally tall and bony. He was so tall that his long legs made it appear as though he was standing on stilts. He wore the black uniform of a German soldier, distinguished by the rank insignia of a Nazi Colonel.

The Oberstfuhrer stared at the boy, admiring the child's perfectly symmetrical face--the child's high cheekbones and square, sturdy chin; the child's creamy-smooth complexion and long, thick eyelashes-features, unlike his own. The Oberstfuhrer's eyes were deeply-set, brown, and listless, between which a long, pointed nose protruded, disfigured by a deep gash down his left nostril. The colonel's hair was muddy brown, thin, and stringy. His skin was pasty-white and spotted with tiny pimples, pink, and peeling. He was an ugly man, not what the Reich considered the ideal Aryan type, which made the Oberstfuhrer's hatred of the Jews even more ferocious.

The second hunter was a short, crusty old doctor named Josef Weiss, with frazzled white hair and large, owl-shaped blue eyes covered by a pair of thick, gold-rimmed spectacles. Denounced by his colleagues as a madman, the doctor's license to practice medicine was revoked. But that was twenty years ago, long before organized insanity spread throughout the country like gangrene infesting an open wound. Today those same colleagues admired and revered the doctor as a medical genius.

The Obertsfuhrer looked on with hungry anticipation as Dr. Weiss stroked the boy's curly blonde hair and opened the child's hallow blue eyes, first the right and then the left. Seven hours ago, the doctor injected four ounces of a serum he invented into the boy's veins.

"How long will it take him to revive?" asked the Oberstfuhrer.

"Three days," answered Dr. Weiss. "The same amount of time it took God to raise Christ from the grave, so the legend goes. According to his age and size, that's the length of time it will take his body to react once the serum has circulated into his bloodstream. For an older man like me, it will take fifteen days, maybe more, for you, five or so."

"But why is there such a difference in the revival time?"

"Because the serum works according to your body's metabolism, so the response time may vary from person-to-person. With each resurrection, the length of death decreases. Also, the quicker the body revives, the less pain the body feels. Consequently, if a person gets stabbed a hundred times, every stab will feel like nothing more than a tiny pinprick. Come! Let me show you."

Strauss followed Dr. Weiss over to the laboratory table and watched closely as the doctor took two rabbits, one white, one brown, out of their cages and placed each in separate metal trays. Dr. Weiss then glanced over at the corner where a young man sat curled against the wall in the fetal position.

"Shoot!" commanded the doctor, pointing to the brown rabbit's head. Slowly struggling to his feet, the young man plodded as quickly as he could towards the rabbit, dragging the weight of his lifeless left foot behind him as the torn and tattered remnants of a blue and white striped prison uniform sagged off his frail and bony body.

The Oberstfuhrer watched the wretched-looking redhead with curiosity.

"A Jewish sympathizer?" Strauss asked.

"No. Worse!" the doctor replied, "a Christian… and my nephew."

Finally reaching the rabbit, the young man fumbled the small pistol tucked inside his pants and held the gun between the brown rabbit's eyes. Trembling, he turned his head away and fired. The rabbit fell dead on the table. The young man let out a frightful moan and then backed away into his corner.

Looking at his watch, Dr. Weiss counted: "…4, 5, 6…."

Holding his breath, the Oberstfuhrer watched as the hole in the rabbit's head rapidly shrank until there was nothing more than a small dent where the bullet entered. Dr. Weiss stopped counting at fifteen. The rabbit sprung to its feet. Reaching into his white coat pocket, the doctor pulled out a carrot and fed it to the rabbit, then glanced over at his nephew.

"See, Hans, see! The rabbit is alive!"

The young man clapped his hands and bobbed his head in jubilation.

"That's my little friend," said Dr. Weiss, patting the rabbit on its head before turning to the Oberstfuhrer.

"As you can see, Kommandant, there is no blood. That's because the instant the bullet punctured the rabbit's flesh, the wound immediately began to heal. In humans, it takes only seconds, once the flesh has suffered a cut, for healing to begin. Now, that process works infinitely faster and better. By tomorrow, the rabbit's body will eliminate the bullet as waste, and in another day or two, the indentation made by the bullet's impact will have disappeared."

As the rabbit sat in the metal tray nibbling on the carrot, the Oberstfuhrer placed the tip of his index finger inside the small dent in the rabbit's head.

"Though undetectable, this rabbit has died many times," said Dr. Weiss. "And with each demise, the length of death decreases, until finally, it will appear as if it never died at all."

"Amazing!" praised the Oberstfuhrer, looking at the rabbit with astonishment. "But how is it possible?" "The serum boosts the composition of the blood cells," explained Dr. Weiss, "enhancing the immune system with a thousand times its usual power to heal itself. Once injected with the serum, the boy's body becomes invincible. Nothing will kill him--- poisons, disease, not even gunshots to the heart! With the immune system so enhanced, the aging process dramatically decreases. But so far, the serum has worked only on male rabbits. Female rabbits injected with the serum have all died. That's because the serum can only be injected into the bloodstream successfully when it's diluted with the male hormone. Testosterone absorbs the serum. Unfortunately, estrogen doesn't. When the testosterone-diluted serum is administered to females, it has the opposite effect. It destroys the blood cells, causing an acute case of Leukemia to develop. The enhanced blood cells have only a one-in-a-million chance of being passed on to female offspring successfully through childbirth compared to a ninety percent success rate for male offspring. So, unfortunately, our frauleins will grow old and die as usual, but German men will have the possibility of living forever."

Reaching under the laboratory table, Dr. Weiss retrieved a blow torch and handed it to the Oberstfuhrer. "What's this all about?" asked the colonel. "You'll see," said Dr. Weiss, picking up the white rabbit and moving it to the far end of the laboratory table. He placed it in a metal cage and then turned to the Oberstfuhrer. "You mean…?

"Yes."

The Oberstfuhrer pressed his finger on the trigger of the blowtorch, engulfing the rabbit and the cage in flames. The rabbit never made a sound, but the Oberstfuhrer cringed as he watched. He coughed, and so did Dr. Weiss as the stench of the metal and burning rabbit fur permeated the air.

Finally, Dr. Weiss motioned to the Oberstfuhrer to stop. When the Oberstfuhrer cut the flare, the cage and the rabbit were as black as tar. Smoke clouded the room as sparks darted from the cage. The rabbit lay dead, burnt to a crisp. Glancing over at the doctor, the Oberstfuhrer noticed him counting again.

"1, 2, 3." Dr. Weiss stopped and moved closer. The Oberstfuhrer did the same and noticed the rabbit's body twitch. Then, suddenly, the rabbit's eyes opened. It lifted its nose to the top of the cage and sniffed. Then, lowering its head, the rabbit took two steps forward before licking the tarred flesh on its feet.

"Mein Got! It's a miracle," the Oberstfuhrer said with both hands pressed against his forehead in disbelief. Unable to contain his excitement, he walked around in circles.

"Wait! Wait! Come here! Quick! Look!"

The Oberstfuhrer returned and watched the color of the rabbit's burnt, black skin rejuvenate itself until all its flesh was pink and healthy again. The Oberstfuhrer could not repress a gasp as he stood with his mouth gaped open.

"Now I dare say, not even God Himself could do better than that!" boasted the doctor, noticeably gushing with pride.

The Oberstfuhrer embraced Dr. Weiss with both arms, grabbing the doctor by the shoulders.

"You are a god!"

"Maybe, but true power comes from the ability to destroy, not just create," said the doctor. Walking back over to the opposite end of the table, the doctor reached his hand over an empty flask and grabbed a bottle of dark brown liquid. Taking another small carrot from his coat pocket, he poured the liquid onto the carrot. The fluid flowed like honey, thick and slow. It even smelled like honey. He then returned to the rejuvenated rabbit and fed the carrot through the burnt metal cage. Seconds later, its flesh darkened until it was black and burnt like before; it lay still, dead again.

"What happened? What did you do?" asked the Oberstfuhrer, looking agitated.

"I fed it the anti-serum, which reverses the effect of the serum. You don't think I would create a serum that gives humans the ability to overcome death without creating an antidote, do you? That would be foolish, insane. For every great man who rises to power, there are two or three lesser men like you who think they are just as great, waiting in the wings to overthrow him. The antidote ensures that such a coup never happens."

The doctor continued. "If any of our loyal comrades no longer want to serve the Fuhrer, getting rid of them will be as easy as feeding them a delicious slice of strudel laced with the anti-serum. Just one bite and snap! They're dead, never to rise again!"

"Once you have killed with the anti-serum, you can't be revived. Whatever the person's wounds were from their many deaths, those wounds will reappear?"

The Oberstfuhrer looked at the charred rabbit. "I see you've thought of everything, doctor." "That's what makes a good doctor great."

Regaining his enthusiasm, the Oberstfuhrer hurried back over to the operating table. "But are you sure the serum will work on humans?" he asked, looking at the dead boy's face.

"Yes," assured Dr. Weiss, rejoining him. "But as I stated before, the serum doesn't work on females."

"Women are of no consequence. Their usefulness lies only in their ability to bear children for the Fuhrer," said the Oberstfuhrer. He then placed his hands back on the doctor's shoulders. "Do you realize what this means? It will make you the most important man in Germany! Perhaps even more important than the Fuhrer himself," said the Oberstfuhrer, also considering the possibilities of his rise to power with a greedy grin of ambition. You will be worshipped and hailed: Vater Hochste--- Father Supreme!"

"Yes, perhaps. But more importantly," said Dr. Weiss, "it will ensure German domination over the world. Just picture it! German soldiers splattered by enemy artillery, yet they keep coming! Nothing the Allied Forces can attack us with can stop us! At such a sight, even our enemies must acknowledge that we are the master race!"

Clasping his hands together behind his back, Dr. Weiss walked pensively over to the arched window. While gazing up at the stars, he closed his eyes for several seconds, then opened them and turned to the Oberstfuhrer.

"Yes, Kommandant Strauss, I must confess that my dream has always been to become the greatest physician the world has ever known. The doctor who gave his countrymen the one extraordinary gift that even God Almighty Himself could not give."

"World supremacy?" asked the Oberstfuhrer

"No," said Dr. Weiss. "Eternal life!"

CHAPTER TWO

"The craving for power becomes
insatiable and limitless when
it gets hold of a
soul that is not master of
itself."

Andrzel Frycz-Modrzewski

"Any sign yet?"

"No, Oberstfuhrer, not yet," answered the soldier, dropping his binoculars and standing at attention.

"Carry on," said Strauss. The Oberstfuhrer gazed down between the columns of the tower wall but could see only the tops of trees clouded in the early morning mist rising from the valley below. The air was crisp and filled with the fragrant smell of pine. Ascending on the horizon was the yellowish-orange glow of a new day. Even from here, the faint rattle of mortar fire and enemy bombs could be heard from hundreds of miles away.

All of Germany was under siege. It was on this day, the morning of April 30, 1945, that Colonel Otto Strauss and a squadron of German soldiers watched and waited for the man they swore to live and die for;

the man who lifted the entire German nation from the abyss of economic despair and political disgrace. To them, and to most of their county men, Adolf Hitler was not a man; he was the Messiah, their Fuhrer-- God. Strauss walked about the open rampart of the tower, occasionally peering down toward the road. His hands were cold, yet sweat dotted his brow as his heart raced. He strained to concentrate, pacing back and forth, continually checking his watch. It was five o'clock in the morning. Soon it would be daylight.

He hurried away to inspect the Fuhrer's sleeping quarters again for the fourth time that morning.

The room was as large as a ballroom with walls covered in light blue silk; a white marble fireplace dominated the east wall. Strauss walked about the bedroom, scrutinizing everything. He rearranged the chairs more than once. He removed the full-length, cheval glass dressing mirror three times from the corner opposite the gold-trimmed bureau chest and placed it beside the Louie XIV bed. Now he put it back again. This time he left the room and was finally convinced that everything was perfect. If Eva Braun, Hitler's mistress, accompanied the Fuhrer, Strauss prepared an adjoining suite. He planned everything down to the smallest detail.

With his promotion to colonel and chief administrator and head of the Lebensborn Society just three weeks ago, Strauss dreamed of becoming part of the "inner circle" in the Wehrmacht, who Hitler confided in and trusted with his life, men like Heinrich Himmler, Head of the Gestapo and Joseph Goebbels, Minister of Propaganda. It was the

Colonel's opportunity to prove himself worthy. He wanted nothing to go wrong.

Returning to his quarters, Strauss paced the floor, rehearsing and re-rehearsing his welcome speech. To think that in an hour from now, he would be in the presence of the Fuhrer. Hitler himself would be sitting across from him at the breakfast table, and tonight, the boy would awaken, and a new era in German history would begin.

Last year, all seemed lost when American and Allied troops landed on the shore of Normandy, and Since then, many of the Lebensborn Homes had been abandoned. Since mid-January, Hitler had been barricaded inside his concrete bunker in Berlin, fifty feet underground.

Strauss spoke to Hitler via radio link just before he arrived four days ago. Despite the advancement of Allied troops, the Fuhrer's secretary gave his word that Hitler would be here to witness the birth of the new world order. It was all arranged. As a safety precaution, Hitler, escorted by his aides, would travel at night incognito through the back roads, forests, and fields to arrive here this morning. Dr. Weiss prepared a full report of his experiments, which Strauss would present to the Fuhrer. To celebrate Germany's annual Day of National Labor, the two American Negro soldiers captured on the battlefield in France would be executed as a tribute to the Fuhrer.

His eyes beamed as Strauss gazed down upon the forest from his bedroom chamber off the east wing. In his mind, he saw a vision of himself adorned in a black uniform. On his sleeve was a white swastika, the symbol of the Nazi Party. Assembled outside was the entire German army. For miles and miles, every officer and soldier in the military lined the streets of Gendarmenmarkt Square in Berlin. They stood in salute before the magnificent Schauspielhaus Theater to watch as Hitler decorated him with the party's highest honor, the Star of the Grand Cross of the Iron Cross. Soon, he would be a general.

Please with himself, Strauss watched from his balcony as the first rays of sunlight sprinkled its soft, yellow glow over the valley. He never dreamed his life would turn out so well. Otto never thought he would rank so high in the world's most feared and powerful army, having completed only intermediate school. When the Nazi Party won the election in 1933, he was sixteen years old and in prison for robbing and killing a wealthy Jewish banker. He still had nightmares about prison.

Forever etched in his memory was the morning he woke up to the beady eyes of a giant black rat sitting on his chest, staring him in the face while another rodent was biting into his leg. He screamed, and the rat on his chest sunk its teeth into the side of his nose and wouldn't let go. A guard heard his cries and rushed into the cell and knocked the rats away with a nightstick before shooting them. Otto almost lost part of his nose and had to get twenty stitches. Fortunately, his prison sentence was cut short. The following year, in a secret mandate, Hitler released all Germans sentenced for killing Jews. Killing a Jew was no longer to be considered a crime.

A month after his release, on May 1, 1933, young Otto swore an oath of allegiance to Adolf Hitler and became a Nationalwast Sozialwastwasche Deutsche Arbeiterpartie member. He enlisted into the Schutzstaffel, Hitler's internal security force, the feared SS. Unlike other boys his age who first became a brown-shirted Hitler youth, Strauss, having spilled Jewish blood, was considered worthy of becoming a full-fledged Nazi.

As an SS soldier, Otto felt he found his niche. He felt his life now had direction and purpose. Otto liked being a Nazi and the power and authority that came with it. He often submitted ideas to his superiors on how to eliminate the Jews, but he earned his reputation for spotting physical characteristics of Jewish ancestry among his fellow Nazi brethren. Otto was so successful that he was feared and avoided by other SS soldiers and had no friends. He didn't care; their fear made him feel important and in control. The ability catapulted him up the ranks, and he became a sergeant by eighteen. A week after turning twenty, Otto accused thirteen soldiers of being Jews and was promoted to lieutenant one month later. In a report addressed to Himmler, Otto gave evidence of the soldier's Jewish heritage by noting their high foreheads, long hook noses, and large-lidded, round eyes.

The next incident, which resulted in his promotion, could have ended badly for Otto, but he got lucky. Out of jealousy, he stabbed an officer in the back and was made a captain when he claimed the officer was a British spy. It just so happened, unbeknownst to Otto, the officer's mother was British, and the soldier had spent several years in an English boarding school. That was proof enough for the Gestapo.

Preibus Gooding was a well-liked lieutenant who was almost as tall as Otto. The lieutenant had piercing green eyes, thick, wavy black hair, a square cleft chin, and a muscular physique. He was the most handsome man Otto had ever seen. Otto envied everything about him, from the lieutenant's highbrow air and polite manners to his uniform's crisp, tailored fit. Gooding survived the stabbing to the back of his shoulder, but after a brutal interrogation by the Gestapo, the lieutenant confessed. Gooding was executed three months later. Executions had become routine and usually done in a nearby town in public view with a narrow trench leading to a large ditch dug in an open field. Otto remembers that day well because it was on June 5, his twenty-second birthday.

It was a breezy, overcast morning. Otto remembered thinking it would rain and regretted not riding in a covered vehicle. He sat smug and proud in his jeep, his chin out and his peaked cap squarely positioned on his head. On his collar was the captain's insignia--a black-and-silver piped patch with three silver embroidered gilt-metal pips and silver Litzen. He looked at no one but sat tall, grinning with self-importance. Eagerly, he waited like a child anticipating the start of an outdoor puppet show, the kind he loved as a boy. Executions usually took place in groups of five. Today, however, there were to be only three.

A military truck transporting Lieutenant Gooding drove up. If it weren't for his green eyes, Otto wouldn't have recognized Gooding. The lieutenant stumbled out of the back of the truck wearing a dirty, blue, and white striped prison uniform with an inverted red triangle sewn on his shirt. Printed on the triangle was the letter B for British. Gone was Gooding's thick, wavy black hair and smooth pink skin. Black, purple, and red bruises now blotted his face and bald head. Dried blood stained his swollen lips. The Lieutenant hobbled down the narrow trench, bent over like a decrepit old man, stopping frequently and swaying back and forth and from side to side.

"Run!" ordered Senior Lance Corporal Alf Gundersen, overseeing the execution. He pushed Gooding and the two other prisoners down the trench with the butt of his rifle. The three ran. The other two made it to the large channel and jumped in, but right before Gooding reached the ditch, he tripped and fell to his knees. Gundersen, a mean burly fellow, a prizefighter before the war, raised his large-booted right foot high off the ground and kicked Gooding so hard in the butt it propelled the lieutenant several feet through the air. The lieutenant's body hit the dirt wall on the far side of the ditch and dropped into the six-foot-deep hole like a swatted fly.

Otto laughed, as did the other soldiers.

Gasps came from the public. A small crowd of twenty-five, consisting mostly of men, was present.

"Let's get on with it," said a man in the crowd. Otto glanced over at the old man, who looked to be in his sixties. The husky German held a rifle and wore a black patch over one eye. Standing beside him were two other civilians with guns, about the same age. It was customary for several of the town's people to join in the execution. It was considered an honor to rid the fatherland of its enemies, and it was a way for those unable to fight in the war to contribute to the cause of the Third Reich and show their allegiance.

Once Gundersen gave the command, the husky old man fired first. The two other men to be executed were Polish political prisoners, as signified by the inverted red triangle and the letter P printed on their prison shirts. The husky old man shot one of the Polish prisoners dead center between the eyes. He stepped aside to let the other two civilians take their shots. The following Polish prisoner was shot once through the heart.

The last executioner stepped forward to shoot Lieutenant Gooding. He lifted his rifle and aimed but didn't fire. Lieutenant Gooding was still on his knees, leaning against the far wall of the ditch, where he fell with his back to the crowd.

"Stehen Sie Sie schmutziger britischer Schaum auf. Stehen Sie auf!" yelled Gundersen. The senior lance corporal called Lieutenant Gooding British scum and ordered him to stand.

Gooding dug his fingertips into the dirt wall and, after several attempts, pulled himself up. He stood trembling and turned to face the crowd.

"Ich bin nicht britisch. Ich bin deutsch. Ich bin ein Nazi. Hitler ist mein Fuhrer. Ich bin nicht ein Spion. Bitte! Bitte! Ich bin deutsch." The condemned lieutenant spoke in a raised, cracked voice, proclaiming his innocence and his allegiance to Hitler. Gooding then lifted his arm and pointed to Otto. He glared at Otto with red, teary eyes, shaking his finger.

Suddenly, gunfire rang out, then another gunshot and another in rapid succession. The shots weren't coming from the civilian executioner. Instead, the eyes of the soldiers and everyone else in the crowd were on Otto standing up in his jeep with smoke curling from the barrel of the pistol in his hand.

"Ha, ha, ha," laughed Lieutenant Gooding. All three shots had missed.

Otto sweated. He was not an excellent marksman. *You Fool! You should have never fired in the first place, scolded the voice inside his head.* Otto's hand shook. He knew he had to shoot again and dare not miss. He hesitated.

"Shoot! Kill him!" shouted Gundersen, peering at Otto sternly, as was everyone else.

Otto inhaled. *Stop shaking! Hold your hand steady and aim at his head.*

Otto wiped the sweat from his brow with his coat sleeve.

Slowly now, slowly press your finger against the trigger. That's it. Go ahead. Shoot!

As soon as Otto pulled the trigger, he fell backward, knocked off his feet by the pure intensity of his desire not to miss. The bang from the gun rang so loud in his ears that Otto was sure his eardrums would burst. He cringed, dropped his pistol, then clamped his hands over his ears. To the crowd, it may have appeared that the captain had never fired a gun; he had, but not with everyone watching and expecting him to make the shot. If the truth is known, Otto did not perform such military skills well under pressure or at any other time.

Otto remained slumped in his car seat. He felt weak and drained of energy. He looked up only slightly and could see Gooding in his peripheral vision. The lieutenant was still standing and was laughing even louder now. Another shot rang out. Otto flinched. The laughing stopped.

"Done," he heard Gundersen's gruff voice say.

It rained suddenly, pouring from the sky like a rushing waterfall. The public quickly dispersed. Otto removed his hat and let the rain drench his face, hoping to hide the tears in his eyes. He wanted to leave, but his fingers wouldn't obey his head and start the engine. Instead, Otto sat there until the bodies were buried and every officer departed. Only then was he able to drive away.

That was four years ago. Otto thought he would never receive another promotion. Now, at twenty-seven, he was a colonel, the youngest officer of such high rank in the Wehrmacht. He was often mistaken for a much older man. The misconception was due partly to his position but primarily to his looks. Otto Strauss had the worn, chiseled face of a forty-year-old man. Deep creases in his forehead and tiny lines around his mouth suggested a life filled with fear, doubts, and unsettling thoughts, a man who doubted everything about himself, from his intellectual capabilities to his place in the world. The disturbing thoughts mainly stemmed from his relentless hatred the descendants of an ancient race, a race he hardly knew anything about-- the Jews. His animosity toward those considered God's "chosen people" developed early in his life. As a boy, he despised the wealthy Jewish businessmen whom his mother entertained weekly. His father died of pneumonia when Otto was only eight years old, leaving his mother to care for him and his two-year-old sister, Greta. Those were desperate times.

"Why do you let them hurt you, Mother?" he'd often asked.

"It's not what you think, Otto. Someday you'll understand," was his mother's reply. Otto never understood. He ran away at twelve, leaving the shame of his mother's life behind for good. He quickly adjusted to his wretched existence, combing the German countryside as a petty thief.

"But just look at me now," Otto whispered, grinning with pride.

The sun was high when Otto glanced down at his watch. It was a quarter to seven. Quickly, he rushed to the rampart.

"Do you see him? Are they coming?"

"No, Oberstfuhrer. There is still no sign," said the soldier holding the binoculars. Strauss grabbed the binoculars from the soldier's hands and looked for himself.

The road to the castle and beyond was vacant of even local vehicles. The colonel then turned to his second in command, Lieutenant Strompf. At 36, Lieutenant Strompf was a man of average height and weight with a long, angular face, dark brown hair and eyes, with a mustache identical to the shape and size of the Fuhrer.

"Has there been any word from Berlin?"

"No, Oberstfuhrer. There has been no contact from any command post for two days, not since I reported the communications malfunction. Our altitude may be interfering with the radio transmission."

Strauss let out a frustrated sigh. What if the Fuhrer doesn't come? It would ruin all his plans. He could feel a headache coming on; the rats were biting again. "I suggest we send some soldiers down to the village. The reception will be better there, and maybe they will be able to contact Berlin," said Lieutenant Strompf.

"Yes! Yes! That's a good idea. Send three men. And as soon as there is news, one should travel ahead with the news."

Lieutenant Strompf saluted with a click of his heels before hurrying away.

It was later that afternoon before a soldier returned. Colonel Strauss was sitting in the dining room, eating lunch. Seated to his left was Dr. Weiss. Lieutenant Strompf and Private First Class Arnulf Kragen entered and saluted. Private Kragen, 20, had broad shoulders and long arms. He combed his sandy blonde hair, parted on the side. Colonel Strauss immediately detected the soldier's apprehension. There was a sad, stoic look on the private's face. The same look shaded the countenance of Lieutenant Strompf.

"Well?!" asked Strauss.

Private Kragen glanced between the colonel and the doctor before finally forcing out the words.

"Hit-Hit-Hitler is dead, sir. An announcement came over the radio. The Russians have invaded Berlin and taken over the city. The Russians found Hitler's body burned outside Hitler's bunker. Reports say Hitler took cyanide."

Strauss and the doctor's faces were filled with complete horror as the two jumped out of their chairs.

"It's a lie! It's a dirty lie!" Strauss shouted. "It's Russian propaganda, that's what it is! Hitler's not dead. He-he can't be dead! The Fuhrer is invincible, indestructible!"

Otto threw the brandy glass in his hand against the fireplace mantel, shattering the gold-framed mirror above it.

Dr. Weiss collapsed back in his chair, shaking his head. "What's going to happen to me? To my experiments?" asked the doctor. "I must hide the serum and burn the formula. No one must know; no one must know what I've done!" screamed Dr. Weiss, rushing out of the room.

Colonel Strauss dismissed his men and paced the floor.

I'm never going to be a general now. What would happen to Germany? Who would lead them? No one could replace Hitler, not even Heinrich Himmler, who had been rumored to have secretly tried to negotiate a surrender to the British. The German army was the most feared and disciplined in the world. They needed someone strong in stature and in speech to lead them, but who?

As Strauss walked toward the fireplace, bits of broken glass crunched beneath the soles of his highly polished black boots. He looked down and caught sight of his reflection in one of the large pieces of broken mirror. Strauss stood a dominating six feet, four inches tall. Strauss had always been proud of his height; it was the one thing he genuinely liked about himself. His right eye twitched as his heart pounded loudly in his ears. A plan was forming in his mind; a vision was emerging, and he reasoned --was not his life and Hitler's almost identical? Had not both served time in the same prison in Landsberg? Had not both rose up from humble beginnings through the ranks of the Wehrmacht? And, even more important, were not both Austrian-born Germans? Yes, yes, yes. What was to stop him from succeeding Hitler as Chancellor of the Third Reich?

With a renewed sense of purpose, Strauss hurried to his quarters. He had to think. What would the Fuhrer do? Everything must proceed as planned. Time was his enemy. Strauss summoned Dr. Weiss to his chamber.

"Dear, Doctor Weiss, tell me. Is there any way to hasten the process of the serum?"

"You mean speed up the resurrection? Well, I suppose if I increase the dose. But I'm almost certain that would cause permanent death."

"That's a chance we'll have to take. Once the boy has awakened tonight, I want you to proceed to give the serum to my men and me. Enough so that we will awaken the next day."

"The next day---Mein Got! That's murder! Besides, I don't have enough for all your men. Making the serum takes time. I only have enough serum on hand to inject thirteen soldiers, and increasing the dosage that much is far too risky."

"I assure you, it's the only way to save the Reich. Now that Hitler is dead, German defeat is a certainty." Strauss pointed to his desk to a map of Austria and Germany.

"The word from high command is that Allied Forces are advancing from all directions. From the Western Front, American troops broke through our west wall defensive position along the Siegfried line and penetrated as far as Bavaria, no doubt working their way toward Austria to meet the Russians. Your serum is the only thing that can save us now. According to military estimates, it will take the Americans at least three to four days, maybe five, to meet up with the Red Army. If your serum works and the process speeds up, once my men revive, we will travel to Austria and be ready and waiting for them by the time the Allied Forces arrive on May 5. My soldiers and I will then be able to halt the Allied Forces' momentum, snatching victory out of the hands of defeat."

"What if you're unable to reach Austria in time?" asked Dr. Weiss

"The serum still assures us victory. Even if we should lose the war, it would only be temporary. For what authority do the dead have over the living?"

There was a knock on the door.

"Come in," said Colonel Strauss.

Lieutenant Strompf entered and saluted. "I have informed the men per your instructions," said Lieutenant Strompf.

"Good! Good!" said Strauss.

"What about the American Schwarze Soldaten?" the lieutenant asked.

"Black soldiers! There're black soldiers here?" Dr. Weiss looked nervously about the room.

"No need to be frightened, doctor. They are in the keep and safely secured. I had planned a grand execution with the Fuhrer looking on, but things have changed. Perhaps you would like to perform one of your mind-altering experiments on them. It should prove very interesting."

Colonel Strauss turned to the lieutenant. "Bring the soldiers to the tower after sundown."

CHAPTER THREE

"For what benefit will it be to a man if he
gains the whole world
but forfeits his soul?"

Matthew 16: 26
New World Translation of the Holy Scriptures

Josef Weiss gathered all the documents on the serum and the report he would present to Hitler and burned them in the fireplace in his bedroom. They were only copies. The originals were hidden in his underground laboratory in Switzerland.

Weiss then slowly walked over to the four-poster bed. The doctor eased his body down on the edge of the bed, took off his glasses, rubbed his eyes, and then his side. The pain was getting worse. He was tired and wanted to nap before sundown, but too many thoughts flooded his mind. The pain he felt wasn't just from terminal cancer that was consuming his body. The pain was also from the haunted memories of his twin brother Johann, his son Olaf, and his two wives. He had failed them all--his brother in his resentment and blind allegiance to Hitler, his wives and son, in his obsession with the serum.

Hans was the only family he had left. Four weeks ago, after a long search and considerable expense, he rescued the poor lad from the Flossenburg labor camp.

The Christian beliefs of his brother and his sister-in-law led to their execution at a concentration camp in Niederhagen in 1943. Hans was just sixteen-years old. Like his parents, Hans wouldn't pledge allegiance to the Nazi party or join the army and suffered tremendously for it. His nephew was brutally beaten almost to death. The trauma impaired his speech and caused some brain damage. He was made to stand naked in sub-zero temperatures in the snow and labored from sun up to sundown on tiny rations of bread and water. But the lad endured and could not stay alive but maintain his faith. It was a faith Josef didn't understand.

Despite being identical, he and his brother were not alike. Johann was the oldest, born three minutes ahead of him. Both were geniuses, but in a different way. Johann's was wise. He could judge complex issues and come up with a moral and just solution. Their father always said Johann had the Wisdom of Solomon. He cared about people, animals, and the condition of the world. He was a quiet man and always accommodating to others, even strangers. Everyone who met Johann liked him. He had a way of connecting with people and empathizing with them. Josef was just the opposite. He cared little for people, especially those he thought were not as smart as he. Math and science were his passions. As a child, Josef was interested in anatomy. He wanted to know what the body looked like inside and how it worked. When Josef was nine, he begged his father to buy him a rabbit for Christmas. His father did, and he cut the rabbit open. Johann called him a murderer and cried for a week. From that day on, there was a distance between them.

Over the years, the distance grew, fueled by Josef's perception that their parents loved his brother more than him. He secretly resented Johann for it.

Once Hitler came into power, he no longer had to hide his disdain. Niceties and love of fellow man, even for one's blood, were replaced with a solid defense for the German Cause and starch loyalty to Hitler. Any German who wasn't for the Third Reich was an enemy.

That was Josef's mindset the day his brother came to him for help in the summer of 1941. Johann wanted to leave and take his family to Canada. His nephew was to turn Fourteen in the fall. His brother and wife, Marta, had conceived Hans late in their marriage after years of trying. Johann came to him in the dead of night at the estate owned by his second wife, Gitta, in Hamburg. He had received a letter from his brother four days earlier requesting to see him.

"Why have you come to see me so late?" Josef stood, holding the front door slightly open. His brother, dressed in all black, looked nervous, fumbling with the hat in his hand.

"I'm so sorry, brother, for disturbing you at such an hour," Johann said, " but this was the safest time we could travel."

Josef peered over his brother's shoulder at the automobile in the driveway. It was too dark to see their faces, but he knew it was Marta and Hans.

"What do you mean the safest time? Is someone after you?"

"Well, I think you know I have been arrested several times, both Marta and I, for our Christian neutrality."

"It's only a matter of time before they arrest us for good and send us to a concentration camp. Most of our brothers and sisters in the faith have been arrested already."

"What do you want me to do about it?"

"I was hoping you would give me the money, the equivalent of nine thousand U. S. dollars, for the passage for the three of us to sail to Canada. The ship sails tomorrow night. The captain will only accept cash in U.S. currency."

Josef had the money to pay the passage a thousand times over.

"No! If you have so much faith in your religion, your God, you shouldn't have to worry about being sent to a concentration camp. Your God should protect you. Furthermore, if you want to go to Canada, your God should provide you with the money."

The sound of him slamming the door in his brother's face haunts him to this day, surpassed only by the screams of his son Olaf. Josef shook his head.

My dear brother, forgive me.

He leaned back on the pillow. An image of Olaf flashed in his head. He could see his son in his mind's eye as clearly as he could see the young soldier standing before him now.

"Excuse me, doctor, the Kommandant requests your presence in the tower, sir."

Josef quickly rose. He put on his glasses and straightened his clothes, then glanced out the window. It was twilight.

"What is your name, young man?

"Dag Narvik, sir." The boy smiled. He was a good-looking lad with dimpled cheeks, blonde hair, and blue eyes. The Nordic ideal the Reich coveted.

"You wouldn't mind if an old man leaned on you a little?"

"No, sir."

Josef linked arms with the young soldier and headed for the tower.

CHAPTER FOUR

Everything that we see is a shadow
cast by that which we do not see.

Martin Luther King, Jr.

From an elongated slot in the outer wall of the keep, an unshaven, thick, and wooly-haired American Negro soldier named Kapp Johnson partially glimpsed the moon. Otherwise, the place was pitch black, cold, and damp. The air was thick and smelled moldy. Kapp imagined himself in a dungeon or some underground cavern and wondered how many other American soldiers had been held prisoners here.

He groaned, still feeling the enemy's fist in his ribs. He tried to shift his weight to relieve the pressure on his aching left hip, but with his feet tied together and both hands secured behind his back, the best he could do was scoot a little to the right.

Out of the darkness came the frightened voice of Private Paul Penson.

"What do you think they'll do to us, Kapp?" Kapp groaned again.

"The same damn thing they do to us back home; whatever the hell they want, just as long as we're dead in the end," Kapp grumbled.

Kapp immediately regretted speaking so bluntly. Pauley was his stepbrother and had just arrived from Fort Bragg training camp three months ago. He was only sixteen, too young to be so far away from home and much too young to see so much killing, death, and destruction. Hell! He was also! Kapp was only twenty-three himself. They were members of the all-black 761st Tank Battalion, which had a tag named "Patton's Panthers," after General Patton. The unit had the reputation of being the best tank fighters in the U.S. Army.

They should have been the best. While white battalions were sent overseas after only two or three months of training, they had trained for over two years before deployment. Racism was the reason for the delay. Most American military leaders had reservations about using Negro soldiers in combat. However, General Lesley J. McNair, commander of Army Ground Forces, successfully argued that Negros should be in combat in segregated units. The 761st was rated "superior" and deemed "combat- ready," after a special review by General Ben Lear,

U.S. Army Commander.

The unit landed in France on October 10, 1944, consisting of six white officers, thirty black officers, and six hundred and seventy-six black enlisted men. At General Patton's request, they were assigned to General Patton's Third Army. Kapp still remembers the speech Patton gave standing on the hood of a half-track, multipurpose vehicle with his fists planted on his hips and his feet spread apart. The general wore a brown mid-length Eisenhower Jacket and pale riding britches.

Strapped to his waist was a brass-buckled gun holster holding two ivory-handled pistols. Patton's boots were shiny enough for Kapp to see his reflection. When Patton spoke, every soldier and officer froze in place and didn't breathe until the general finished.

"Men, you're the first Negro tankers to ever fight in the American Army. I would never have asked if you weren't good. I have nothing but the best in my Army. I don't care what color you are. Everyone has their eyes on you and is expecting great things from you. Most of all, your race is looking forward to your success. Don't let them down, and damn you, don't let me down."

Colonel John Baker was the commander of the 761st. Baker, An All-American in football, was tall and lean with curly brown hair and brown eyes. He hailed from Berkeley, California, and had no contact with Negros growing up, nor in college, which meant he wasn't tainted with any pre-conceived notions about how Negro's should or shouldn't act. That made him the perfect officer to lead the unit. Kapp liked him, and so did all the other tankers. He was tough but fair and always treated them with respect.

The other five white officers viewed Negros as most whites commonly did. Throughout the war, Kapp noticed a change in some of the white officer's attitudes. It was hard to hate someone when your life depended on them. Kapp saw firsthand there weren't any atheists or racists in foxholes.

Major Timothy Whittlecat was evidence of that. He was what Southern Negros called an "institutionalized cracker." He hailed from Alabama, and everybody knew it when he opened his mouth. Besides speaking with a deep Southern Twang, he had the very Southern custom of calling Negros, coons, and niggers. Colonel Baker was furious when he heard Whittlecat call Lieutenant Taylor the latter. The colonel told Whittlecat if he ever heard him call another officer or any other enlisted man that again, he would have him court-martialed. That didn't stop Whittlecat from uttering the words out of the colonel's earshot.

Kapp laughed when he heard about Colonel Baker's threat, as did every other Colored soldier in the unit. It was highly unlikely that a court-martial of the major would succeed just for calling Negros what most whites in America also called them. But Major Whittlecat stopped using those words after Lieutenant Taylor saved his life.

Lieutenant Milton Taylor was a career soldier nicknamed "Ostrich" because of his long, skinny neck. Despite being from the Southside of Chicago, the lieutenant's easy-going disposition served him well in the army. Even in the worst situations, Lieutenant Taylor always found a bright side. When given a mission, Taylor focused on the task and blocked out everything else until the job got done. The day he saved Major Whittlecat's life was no different.

It was the first time the 761st saw action in the "Big Offensive." The 26th Infantry Division was to fight on the high ground in a small village surrounded by rolling hills south of Chateau-Salins in northeast France. The order came down that the 761st was to lead the attack. The unit was to support the advancement of ground troops, light tanks, and other medium tanks by direct fire. They were to observe the enemy and develop weak spots. Assist the infantry in destroying pillboxes and taking out enemy weapons.

It was a cold, gray November morning. It had been raining most of the night, and there was still a drizzle when daylight broke through the clouds. The terrain was a muddy mess dotted with standing pools of water. Slowly, the 761st rolled their tanks into attack formation, settled down, and waited, some perched on hills shouldered between giant trees and large bushes, others in open view.

The tanks commanded by Major Whittlecat, Lieutenant Taylor, and Kapp sat on a steep slope, with Kapp flanked on the left, Major Whittlecat flanked farthest to the right, and Lieutenant Taylor in the middle.

The Germans fired the first shot. A sudden blast from an 88mm was sharp and piercing. The explosion was so loud Kapp could still hear ringing in his ears two days later. The shell exploded high in the sky, far off to the right, billowing up in a mushroom of smoke beyond the reach of Major Whittlecat's tank. Still, shortly after the explosion, Lieutenant Taylor yelled to the major to take cover as if he knew a piece of shrapnel had the major's name on it and would strike the major's turret just as the major was about to lower his hatch. Shrapnel hit Major Whittlecat's tank with such force; it sent him flying through the air and over the cliff.

Lieutenant Taylor radioed firing instructions to all the gunners: "Tanks—AP—Traverse Right— Range: 235—Fire!"

Every tank on the cluster of surrounding hills fired. As the artillery duel with the Germans began, Taylor climbed out of his hatch and searched for the major. He found Whittlecat lying halfway down the hill unconscious, an easy target for a sniper. Taylor hoisted the major over his shoulder and hauled him up the cliff. He then carried Whittlecat behind the firing line to safety. After that, Kapp never heard nigger or coon uttered from the major's mouth again.

Still, one whitey's conversion couldn't justify why he and Pauley were in a foreign country, risking their lives to help one white man kill another. Neither of which gave a rat's ass about Negroes. Back home, People of color had to ride in the back of the bus if they could ride at all. They were paid less for doing the same jobs as whites. They were segregated, castrated, hunted down like wild animals, shot, and lynched.

"What if they torture us?" asked Pauley out of the blue. "I'm not afraid to die. One shot in the head, and it's all over. But torture. I'm scared I'll crack. That I'll say something or…" His stepbrother's voice fluttered and then faded.

"Don't worry, if they don't suspect we're related, it'll be all right. So don't say anything that would lead them to believe we are more than just soldiers. Otherwise, they might try to use it against us," said Kapp. "Don't be afraid, Pauley. Just remember, whatever they tell you to do, don't do. Moreover, whatever they ask you--don't answer. Listen, keep talking, and I'll try to slide over to you."

Finally, after several minutes, Kapp maneuvered his way over to his stepbrother. "Here I am. Now lay your head on my shoulder," said Kapp in a fatherly tone.

Pauley obeyed.

"That's it. Rest easy now. Just close your eyes and think of Mama."

Kapp had a better view of the full moon from here. Seeing it reminded him of summer nights back home in Georgia, where he could look up and see clusters of twinkling, blue stars winking down at him from heaven. "Diamonds in the sky," went the nursery rhyme. There was nothing like hot summer nights in River Ben, with the sweet, syrupy fragrance of peach blossoms caressing your nostrils and the joyful sounds of children laughing as they played tag and hide n' seek.

Kapp thought about all his childhood friends who had never reached adulthood. Ray Cooper drowned when he was ten-years-old by a gang of white schoolboys who wanted to see how long Ray could hold his breath underwater. There was his cousin Floyd, fourteen, who was stabbed on the road by one of the local white trash for accidentally brushing up against a white girl in town the day before. Curtis Witherspoon had been missing for almost two months before his folks found him in the woods hanging from a tree. Curtis was seventeen. There was....

Kapp knocked the back of his head against the stone wall to banish the ghosts from his mind. The face of his wife Clara flashed before his eyes--soft, slender Clara who walked with all the pride and grace of a gazelle. Clara dreamed of becoming a ballerina, but she had to settle for being a nurse instead. Negroes don't have the physical stamina for classical ballet, the white instructors told her. Poor Clara, she would never be what she wanted to be. Kapp had been one of the lucky ones and attended Morris Brown College on an athletic scholarship and studied physical education. He dreamed of being a coach of a college football team. Kapp liked coaching more than playing. He would have started his first year as an Assistant Athletic Instructor at Howard University if America hadn't declared war and he hadn't volunteered. Damn!

As Kapp watched daylight slowly surrender to the night, a lump formed in his throat while a gnawing feeling grew inside his stomach. It was a feeling he knew all too well: fear. Kapp had survived growing up in the mire of racial hatred that permeated the Deep South. But how would he ever escape from here, the hollow pit of Gehenna? Kapp knew he would never see his beloved Clara again. In the background, he could hear the steady clip-clap of footsteps getting louder as they approached. While gazing up at the stars, Sergeant Johnson closed his eyes and made a wish.

CHAPTER FIVE

"A member of the SS must be decent, fit,
loyal, and a good comrade to his fellows, but not
towards representatives of other
countries….They (other people) interest me only
to the extent that we need them as slaves for our
culture. We Germans, who are the only people in
the world who have a correct attitude towards
animals, will also have a proper attitude towards
these animal human beings."

Heinrich Himmler, October 4, 1943.

Black Forest, Sundown, April 30, 1945

The main room of the castle tower was large, with
thick wooden crossbeams supporting a high-vaulted
ceiling. Lanterns hung from each of the stone walls.
Several relics of medieval knight's armor stood against
them. Fixed to the walls around the room were shields
and crossbows of axes and swords. Positioned in the
center of the room, cluttered with bottles, flasks, tubes,
and burning candles, was the doctor's laboratory table.
Behind the desk, a tall arched window reached twelve
feet from the floor from which the light of the full

moon cast an eerie glow. To the left of the laboratory table hung a long black velvet curtain covering a door to a smaller chamber where the body of the ten-year-old Polish boy lay dead. Just right of the stairs, on the opposite side of the room, was a corner nook where the doctor's nephew, Hans, slept.

Colonel Strauss heard footsteps ascending the stairwell and braced himself as he stood beside the lab table. He felt a prickly sensation crawling up the back of his neck and tried to wipe the feeling away several times with the handkerchief in his hand, but the tinkling remained. Strauss was anxious and didn't know why seeing two chained and guarded Negro prisoners made him so nervous. Though he had never seen Negros before except for in American-made films, he had seen the two coming up the stairs now at the Dulag facility in Berlin where he first saw them from a distance standing in the prison yard. He was told about their capture by Lieutenant Strompf and requested they be transported here for a ceremonial execution. Soon the Negroes would be in the same room with Strauss, face-to-face, and no matter how often he told himself not to be, the prospect made the colonel uneasy. He wasn't alone. The colonel glanced over at Dr. Weiss. The doctor was fidgeting with his hands and pacing the floor back and forth.

Like a rabbit trying to find its way through a maze, Dr. Weiss scampered about, taking only a few steps before changing directions—right, walk, walk, left, walk, walk, reverse, and repeat.

The first sight of Kapp, as he stepped up from the stairwell, sent a shiver down the colonel's spine.

Kapp's hairy face and bushy hair made the black soldier appear every bit as menacing as Colonel Strauss imagined a Negro man to be, and the words "black ape" immediately came to mind.

As the two American soldiers, escorted by four of his men, were led to him, Strauss backed away, not wanting to get too close. He merely pointed to the chairs where the prisoners were to sit and didn't speak. His throat was dry; his tongue stuck to the roof of his mouth.

Dr. Weiss rushed over and stood behind the colonel.

"Huh hmm," Strauss cleared his throat several times and stood far away. Minutes passed before he finally mustered up the courage to speak.

"I am Colonel Otto Strauss of Hitler's Internal Security Force, and this is Josef Weiss, the world's most brilliant physician and scientist."

Dr. Weiss peeked from behind the colonel's back at the two Negro soldiers now seated side-by-side with their backs to the arched window, facing Strauss. Each was strapped to a chair with their arms wrapped around the back end of the chair and their wrists tied tightly together. The hairy one sat to the right of the colonel. The other one, a lanky, light-skinned soldier with small black button eyes and woolly light-brown hair, sat to the colonel's left. The skinny soldier looked a lot younger than the hairy one and to Strauss, far less threatening.

"Now that we've introduced ourselves," said Colonel Strauss, clasping his hands together nervously, "it's your turn."

The colonel stepped toward Private Penson. "Tell me, young soldier, what is your name?"

Private Penson's lips quivered as he stared straight ahead. He didn't speak or even look at the colonel.

"Come, come now! No need for such stiff silence. We are all friends here. No one will hurt you if you cooperate," Strauss grinned. The fear on the young soldier's face made the colonel's blood tingle, and his prior apprehensions vanished. Leaning in closer, Strauss whispered into the young soldier's ear. "Tell me your name and the names of your commanding officers, and I'll let you go," said the colonel in a kind voice. He circled clockwise around the private's chair, then back around in the opposite direction.

Pauley remained silent.

"Your name!" Strauss sneered. "What is your name?" Boom! "Tell me your name?" Boom! Boom! Strauss kept stumping his foot on the floor as hard as he could, trying to frighten the young soldier even more. Pauley just blinked several times but still wouldn't answer. The colonel detached the black leather strap from the clip on his belt and struck the private hard across the face.

"Leave him alone, you stinking, murdering Nazi!" Kapp shouted, tugging and twisting the ropes around his hands to break free.

Strauss immediately switched his attention to Kapp.

"Ahh, and who do we have here, an officer perhaps; maybe a sergeant?"

With new-found confidence and an air of superiority, the colonel strutted over to the hairy black soldier and stood directly in front of Kapp.

"Yes, I think so," said Strauss, noticing the stripes on Kapp's sleeves. "For surely, such a display of raw animal aggression had to be taught. It is common knowledge that the Negro mind is much too far down on the evolutionary pole to react in any other manner than that of whiny little mice." Strauss bent over until he and the sergeant were eyeball-to-eyeball. "Isn't that right, nigger!" Strauss taunted.

Kapp drew back his head and squawked. A big glob of spit landed between the colonel's eyes.

"There's your nigger!" Kapp shouted.

Two German soldiers immediately pounced on Kapp, striking him repeatedly in the face and stomach while Strauss frantically wiped the spit from the bridge of his nose with his handkerchief.

Dr. Weiss assisted the colonel by rushing over to his laboratory table and pouring rubbing alcohol on a cotton swab to disinfect the area.

Finally, Colonel Strauss raised his hand.

"That's enough! We don't want to beat him to death. That's much too dignified an end for him. The two of them must die like the rodents they are—like rats, vile, hideous rats that must be exterminated from the earth before their kind contaminates the rest of humanity." Colonel Strauss walked back over to Kapp, this time keeping his distance. "Yes! You are nothing but a rat, and you're going to die like a rat, squealing and squawking. However, first, you will have the pleasure of watching your comrade die," said Strauss, grinning at Kapp's bruised and bloody face.

Colonel Strauss glanced over at the young private. Pauley still hadn't blinked while continuing to fix his gaze straight ahead.

"Your young comrade will be given a highly potent drug, much like opium, but with far deadlier side effects in which his brains will boil until it shrivels up and shrinks like a prune."

Kapp saw the terrified look on Pauley's face and passed his stepbrother a compassionate glance.

Dr. Weiss injected the needle into the private's arm. Within seconds, the drug took effect, causing Pauley's eyelids to flutter and flick. The young private wiggled in his chair and bolted up and down.

"Fire, fire! I'm on fire! Help Kapp! Help me! I'm burning! My legs are on fire! Put it out! I'm burning! Help Kapp! Help me! Ahhhh!"

Kapp wiggled in his chair, causing it to jolt from side-to-side. He couldn't stand hearing his stepbrother cry for help and being unable to do anything. The screams lasted only a few seconds before all vital signs of life stopped. Pauley looked petrified with his eyes wide open and sunken into their sockets.

Colonel Strauss shook his head from side-to-side. "Tsk, tsk, tsk, poor little mouse, not a very good specimen I'm afraid. Now it's your turn, sergeant."

Dr. Weiss rushed back over to his laboratory table to prepare another needle.

"Hurry, doctor! Quickly!" commanded the colonel.

Anxious and nervous, Dr. Weiss grabbed a vial. His hands shook so rapidly that the glass tube slipped through his fingers and broke into tiny pieces on the floor.

The Kommandant growled at the doctor.

Frantically, Dr. Weiss grabbed another vial from one of the two alabaster cases containing pale red and pinkish-red liquid. This time the doctor forced himself to keep his hands steady as he filled the syringe. Dr. Weiss then turned and walked slowly toward the soldier.

"I'll do it!" blurted the colonel before snatching the syringe out of the doctor's hand.

With a wide, mean grin, Colonel Strauss approached Kapp with a steady and determined gait. Then, just as Strauss was about to plunge the needle into the sergeant's face, Kapp broke loose from the leather straps, jumped up, and lunged at the colonel. Quickly, all four of the Nazi soldiers rushed to restrain the sergeant. After ten minutes of struggling, they finally secured Kapp in the chair again with even more straps tied in tighter knots.

"Hold his head steady," ordered the colonel to his men. Two of the soldiers obeyed, and Strauss rammed the needle into Kapp's cheek with such force that Kapp's chair tipped backward. Thirty minutes passed before the drug took effect. It took that long for Dr. Weiss' breathing to return to normal and for the colonel and his soldiers to relax.

The doctor finally noticed Kapp's eyes squint and blink in rapid succession.

"His brain is beginning to boil now," said the doctor to the colonel.

Colonel Strauss, who was leaning against the laboratory table, walked over to Kapp. "Can you feel the tiny prickles of heat?"

Small beads of sweat drenched Kapp's bearded face. He rubbed his teeth together, making a grating noise to bear the sharp bursts of pain now surging through his veins like currents of electricity.

"The Colored soldier has a strong will," observed the doctor.

"Yes. I'm impressed. Too bad the sergeant isn't German. He would make an excellent candidate for the serum," said the colonel, noticing how the muscles in the Black soldier's arms could be detected even through his shirt. The Oberstfuhrer couldn't help but wonder why God had given such strength, such power to a creature of such low intelligence and not to him. Look at this black brute, this slug of humanity. He has the body of a gladiator: strong, broad shoulders, a muscular neck, long, stout arms, and large, nimble fingers. Even strapped to a chair, he looked formidable. If his kind were allowed to flourish, the Aryan race would be blotted out forever.

Kapp's eyes were now the color of crimson. A red so deep, they blazed like flaming balls of fire. A steady stream of sweat trickled down his swollen, purple cheeks and dripped from his mustache and beard. There was a strange calmness to his countenance. The calm lasted for only a few seconds; then, his breathing erupted into rapid successions of short, sharp pants followed by violent convulsions that twisted and distorted his skin.

Colonel Strauss smiled. Watching the burly soldier fight to live was exhilarating and made him feel all-powerful. Relishing the feeling, Strauss licked his lips, then closed his eyes and inhaled one long deep breath as if sucking in all the power from the room.

Kapp screamed, and Strauss opened his eyes just in time to see the sergeant's head fall forward.

"Yes!" Colonel Strauss yelled in triumph while pumping his fist in the air. He watched as Dr. Weiss checked the soldier's pulse.

"He's dead," the doctor confirmed.

Strauss beamed as he locked his hands together. He then turned to Lieutenant Strompf.

"Remove the rodents and burn their bodies. Come, Dr. Weiss, there's much to be done before the boy awakens tonight," said Strauss as he and the doctor descended the stairwell.

Two of the four German soldiers quickly unstrapped Pauley's body and carried it away as Lieutenant Strompf watched the two soldiers that had beaten Kapp, untie the sergeant. One soldier started with Kapp's hands strapped to the back of the chair, and the other bent down and untied Kapp's ankles. The soldier was loosening the last tied knot around Kapp's ankles when the moaning started.

Lieutenant Strompf and his men first glanced at each other and then at the black soldier. Kapp's body was motionless, and his head bent down into his chest. The lieutenant and his men looked about the dimly-lit room. Lieutenant Strompf then glanced over at Hans, who was sitting quietly in the corner on his cot with his legs crossed.

Lieutenant Strompf shrugged his shoulders and then nodded to his men to continue. They did. A few seconds later, the moaning began again. The soldier kneeling at Kapp's feet jumped up and hurried beside the lieutenant, this time certain the sound had come from the dead soldier. They all stared at Kapp.

"Look! His index finger, it moved," said the soldier, pointing to Kapp's left hand.

"Didn't you see it twitch, sir?" asked the same soldier standing next to the lieutenant.

Lieutenant Strompf didn't answer, and neither did the other soldier.

The third moan was undeniable. It was loud and hollow like the bong from a foghorn; it must have come from the sergeant. The lieutenant backed away as did his men. Strompf gently pulled his pistol from his holster. As he raised the gun to the Black soldier's face, Kapp's eyes suddenly opened.

Lieutenant Strompf pulled the trigger. He missed. Within a blink, Kapp jumped out of his chair and knocked the gun out of the lieutenant's hand.

"He's alive! He's alive! Kommandant!"

Lieutenant Strompf hollered, then blew his whistle and ran toward the stairwell. His men ran too. The lieutenant never made it. Kapp stretched out his long muscular arm and grabbed the lieutenant by the neck. With his fingers tightly gripped around Strompf's throat, Kapp squeezed the life from the lieutenant's body.

It was at that moment, as the lieutenant's limp body fell at Kapp's feet, that Colonel Strauss, Dr. Weiss, and the two soldiers that carried Private Penson's body away, rushed up from the stairwell.

Dr. Weiss froze at the sight of the six-foot black giant lurching over the body of Lieutenant Strompf.

"Kill the beast!" yelled the colonel to his men. Surrounding Kapp, the four soldiers rushed him, but couldn't hold him. The first Nazi soldier was knocked unconscious with one blow to the face. Kapp split the skull of the second soldier with a butt to the head and pummeled the last two Nazis with a flurry of punches then hurled them both simultaneously into the laboratory table.

"The serum! The serum! Stop him!" hollered the doctor, watching his lab table slide across the floor toward the wall as the two Germans crumbled to the floor.

Colonel Strauss rushed over to Kapp and tried to punch him in the jaw. But Kapp was too strong and too quick. Blocking the colonel's punch, Kapp maneuvered around the back of the colonel and secured the colonel in a tight headlock. Red flushed the colonel's face as Kapp squeezed and squeezed his big muscular arm around the colonel's puny neck. Colonel Strauss felt his throat burn. No matter how hard he tried, Strauss couldn't break the black soldier's vice-like grip. Humiliated and helpless, tears swelled in the colonel's eyes as he coughed and spat and clawed the air. His resistance was fading. Gasping for breath, Colonel Strauss managed to eke out a cry to Dr. Weiss: "Hel-hel-help me!"

Still standing at the stairwell, unable to move, the doctor finally found his feet. He ran over to his nephew, still sitting on the cot with his arms wrapped around his legs and his head buried between his knees, shaking in fright.

Get up, Hans! Get up! Shoot! Shoot!" yelled Dr. Weiss at the top of his lungs, trying to urge his nephew to stand. Finally, his nephew rose. Hans pulled out the pistol from the tuck of his pants, held it out in front of him, and gradually plodded towards the two men. He stopped just two feet away from Kapp and the colonel.

"Don't just stand there, you fool! Shoot him! Kill him!"

With Kapp's back facing him, Hans slowly pressed his finger against the trigger and fired the first shot, which pierced Kapp's spine. When Hans fired again, Kapp released the colonel and turned around. Kapp stumbled towards Hans. Hans shrieked, backed away, and fired another shot, dead center into Kapp's chest. Kapp staggered backward toward the arched window. Another shot was fired and another. With each bullet that penetrated his flesh, Kapp twisted and turned and backed away, until finally, he crashed through the arched window and fell a hundred feet to the ground below.

Dr. Weiss rushed over to assist Colonel Strauss, who lay nearly strangled on the floor. "Here, let me help you, Oberstfuhrer." Dr. Weiss grabbed the colonel by the arm and tried to lift the colonel to his feet.

"Hans! Help me!" called the doctor in a strained voice. Hans trudged quickly over to Strauss and grabbed the colonel's other arm. Once on his feet, Colonel Strauss pushed Hans away. After straightening his uniform, the colonel looked about the tower. His men were knocked out or dead.

"Get up, you worthless imbeciles! You call yourselves Nazis! A bunch of weak, worthless frauleins is what you are! Get up!"

Strauss walked over to the soldier nearest him and kicked the soldier in the ribs. The soldier groaned and tried to lift his body off the floor but collapsed back down.

Now you see why we need the serum. After years of intense training, this is the result. Our best fighting men squashed like ants by one black ape!"

Minutes later, three more soldiers stampeded up the stairwell with guns drawn. They approached the colonel and saluted, "Heil Hitler!"

"We were patrolling the grounds when we heard shots," said the corporal.

"Everything's under control now. No thanks to your courageous comrades whose combined force was unable to overpower an attack of one drugged monkey," the colonel spit. Colonel Strauss pointed to the smashed window.

"Below, you will find a dead American soldier. Retrieve his body. Cut it up into little pieces and feed the pieces to the dogs!"

The older, dark-haired corporal hesitated, looking at Private First Class Arnulf Kragen and then at young Private Dag Narvik.

"Well, what are you waiting for?"

"But Oberstfuhrer, we've already searched, sir. There is nobody. There's nothing there but broken glass and a few drops of blood," explained the corporal. The colonel and the doctor passed each other a glance, then immediately ran to the window.

"Hand me your flashlight," ordered Colonel Strauss to the corporal. Colonel Strauss clicked on the light and scanned the ground below. He panned the flashlight back and forth along the edge of the castle wall, on the grass, and up and down the gravel pathway, but no matter where he beamed the light, the body of the American Negro soldier wasn't there. Dr. Weiss rushed over to the laboratory table. The Colonel followed and watched as the doctor picked up an empty vial from one of the two alabaster cases. The doctor shook his head and cried out.

"No! No!"

Deducing what had happened, Colonel Strauss slammed the flashlight down on the table.

"How could you have made such a stupid mistake, doctor?"

"As you can see, both the serum and the drug are almost identical in color. However, one is slightly pinker than the other. I did that on purpose. To make it more difficult for someone to steal," said Dr. Weiss, fumbling with his hands.

The Oberstfuhrer stared at the vials in the two alabaster cases. It was hard to distinguish which one was which. The serum in both cases looked red to him. "Well, I say you've achieved that doctor. So much so, it was even hard for you to tell them apart. So what are we to do now?"

"Catch the soldier and feed him the anti-serum, of course," said Dr. Weiss.

"That may be easier said than done," Strauss replied. "You've seen what strength he has. How are we supposed to track the soldier at night in the dense woods of the Black Forest?"

"We must find him. We can't allow him to live," said Dr. Weiss. "If he is allowed to return to America and procreate, given how virile his kind is, the Negro race would someday overtake the world, and our plan of a new world order under German control would be doomed forever."

Strauss gasped and turned to the corporal. "Search the forest at once! Take as many soldiers as you think you'll need, some in jeeps, some on foot, and find that Negro. No excuses, you here! If you don't bring him back, I'll execute the lot of you. Now go!"

"Yes, sir!" The corporal clicked his heels, saluted, and quickly departed.

Colonel Strauss turned to the two remaining soldiers, Arnulf and Dag. "You two carry out Lt. Strompf's body and help the others, then return here to the tower."

CHAPTER SIX

If we must die—let it not be like hogs Hunted and
penned in an inglorious spot, while round us bark the
mad and hungry dogs, making their mock at our
accursed lot. If we must die—oh, let us nobly die, so
that our precious blood may not be shed in vain; then
even the monsters we defy shall be constrained to
honor us though dead!
Oh, Kinsmen! We must meet the common foe;
though far outnumbered, let us show us brave, and
for their thousand blows deal one deathblow!
What though before us lies the open grave?
Like men, we'll face the murderous, cowardly pack,
pressed to the wall, dying, but fighting back.

Claude Mc Kay

The bullets burned like hot coals in Kapp's body as
he darted through the forest with the moon at his back.
One bullet pierced his upper chest, another pierced
his spine, and several penetrated his stomach and
thighs. Still, his blood pulsated, tingled, and twitched
through his veins like a high volt of electricity.

Thump, thump, thump drummed his heart in his
ears. He ran swift and fast, dodging trees, jumping

across ditches and over large fallen tree branches as the crisp night air pumped in and out of his nostrils and the cold, damp earth crunched underneath his bare feet.

"Kaaapp! Kaaapp!"

Kapp slowed at the raspy call of his name. "Kaaaapp! Kaaaapp!"

Kapp stopped and looked about. He was dazed and disoriented. He didn't know where he was or where he was going. However, he knew he wasn't in America. Kapp vaguely recalled crossing an ocean. He remembered standing on a ship staring out at sea, but now he saw only a silhouette of giant trees all around him outlined against a moonlit sky. There were no woods like this back home in Georgia, no night so moody. Kapp peered up at the nickel moon. The shimmer of its fluorescent glow stung his eyes, and he cupped his hands over his face.

Kaaaapp! Kaaaapp!

This time the voice sounded familiar, yet further away as if calling him from the other side of the world. Kapp lowered his hands to his sides and looked about again. The woods had suddenly grown familiar. Night had become day, and Kapp Johnson returned home to River Ben, Georgia.

"Kapp!"

Kapp looked back over his shoulder. His stepbrother, Pauley, was lying on the ground, and Kapp ran back to get him.

"Get up! They are coming!" Kapp shouted as Jimmy Hodges and four other white boys chased them with sticks and baseball bats.

"We've got to get over the fence!"

"I don't think I can, my leg," whined Pauley rubbing his thigh.

"If Jimmy and his gang catch up with us, it won't be just your leg that's hurting. Now come on!"

Kapp jerked Pauley to his feet, then shoved him up and over the wooden fence before he, too, climbed over it himself. He had almost cleared it with one leg straddled over the top when he felt something holding him back. Kapp looked down and saw the hem of his pants leg clutched between the teeth of Jimmy Hodges' mangy greyhound dog, Blue Boy.

"That's right. Hold him Blue Boy! We've got you now, nigger!" shouted Jimmy, still a fair distance away. Kapp shooed away his brother.

"Run! Go on! I'll catch up with you!" Kapp looked back at Jimmy, and a rock about the size of a peach seed clunked him on the one side of his nose, and immediately blood gushed out of his right nostril. The stones kept coming. One bounced off his thigh and popped him on his chin; another nicked his ear. Kapp swung his right leg back over the fence and hopped down. He then reared his free foot and rammed it into Blue Boy's ribs as hard as he could.

The mutt squealed as it flew through the air and hit the ground two feet away. Still lodged between the dog's teeth was a piece of Kapp's pants leg.

Kapp quickly hopped the fence and ran up and over the hill. He could see his house now, just beyond the dirt road. Kapp quickly caught up to Pauley. At sixteen-years-old, Kapp was big and husky. Without breaking his stride, he leaned down and scooped his little brother under his right arm like Pauley was a football, and Kapp was running for a touchdown in his high school game. When Kapp finally reached the house, he didn't stop. He ran inside and grabbed his stepfather's shotgun from behind the icebox.

"If I were you, crackers, I wouldn't come any closer," shouted Kapp, stepping out from behind the screen door onto the front porch while Pauley watched from the parlor window. Kapp pointed his rifle at Jimmy.

Crazy Jimmy just laughed and grinned and jiggled about with his arms spread out like a vulture circling a dead carcass while exposing every rotten tooth in his foul-smelling mouth. Then Jimmy puckered his lips, drew back his head, and spit a wad of tobacco juice the size of a silver dollar on the toe of one of Kapp's brand-new sneakers.

"Go ahead and shoot! And I guarantee my daddy and every white man in town will lynch you and your whole stinking, nigger family!"

"Maybe, but you won't be alive to see it," said Kapp, mimicking the cocky tone in Jimmy's voice. Jimmy stepped forward. Kapp lifted his rifle closer to his face and squinted for a better aim at Jimmy's forehead. Jimmy hesitated, lowered his arms, and spit again. This time, the tobacco juice missed Kapp's sneakers and splattered on the porch steps just below Kapp's feet.

"Come on, let's go," said Jimmy, waving to his gang. "I owe you one, nigger, especially for what you did to Blue Boy!" Jimmy huffed, backing away.

Hours later, as Kapp and Pauley sat on the front porch snapping green beans for supper, Pauley asked why white folks hated them so much.

"Because we're black," said Kapp.

"But that doesn't make any sense," said Pauley. "Black is just a color. Ole man Griffin, whom daddy drives for, doesn't like the color green, cos I heard him say so. But he doesn't go around cutting down all the trees or burning up all the grass. I think there's another reason. I think it's because they're afraid of us."

Kapp smiled. Pauley was a lot smarter than he was at nine-years-old. Kapp was just now figuring that out about white folks himself. When his mother remarried a year ago, Kapp wasn't too happy about it. He resented having to share his mother, especially since Kapp's father had only been dead two years-- shot in the back for trying to organize a union of the Pullman Porters. But since then, Kapp had grown to love both his stepfather and his stepbrother. He couldn't imagine loving his stepbrother anymore, even if they were blood-related.

"Pauley!" Kapp screamed in grief at the top of his lungs.

"Pauley! Pauley!" The shrill of his voice bounced off the trees and echoed through the crisp night air. Kapp's memory of Pauley tied to a chair and screaming returned. He ran back the way he came. Into the moon, Kapp raced as fast as he could, his feet barely touching the ground. He knew where he was now and where he was going. Kapp also knew what he had to do. He was going back to the castle to retrieve Pauley's body and kill the murdering Nazis who killed his baby brother.

CHAPTER SEVEN

"I am the resurrection and the life."
John 11:25

New World Translation of Holy Scriptures

Midnight, May 1, 1945

The boy, lying on the cold steel of an operating table, awakened from death the same way he died screaming. Concealed behind the black velvet curtain in a small chamber in the tower of Burg Rottlen Castle, the boy kicked, yelled, and swung his fists wildly through the air, blocking any attempts by Dr. Weiss to embrace him or to calm him down. Standing nearby, Colonel Strauss and two soldiers, Arnulf and Dag, watched the boy have his tantrum.

Finally, the colonel intervened. He approached the boy and looked him in the eyes with a stern, commanding gaze. The colonel then raised his right arm and barked," Heil Hitler!"

Immediately the boy stopped screaming, jumped off the operating table, and stood up straight.

Imitating the colonel's posture, the boy saluted back and repeated, "Heil Hitler!" before his knees buckled.

"Adok!" Dr. Weiss called out as he and Colonel Strauss quickly grabbed the child before he fell.

"What's his full name, and where is he from?" asked Colonel Strauss.

"His name is Adok Makowski. He is from Slupsk, located in the northwestern part of Poland, near the Baltic Sea. The city is just one hundred and eighty-five miles from the German border." said the doctor.

The two led Adok back to the operating table and sat him down.

"He needs food," Dr. Weiss stated.

Colonel Strauss ordered Private Narvik to bring the boy something to eat.

CHAPTER EIGHT

"Suffer little children,
and forbid them not to come to me: for of
such is the kingdom of heaven."

Matthew 19:14
American King James Version

Adok wasn't hungry, but he felt compelled to eat. He didn't crave his Mother's homemade croquettes, or the taste of pierogi, his favorite dish. Still, he stuffed his mouth with everything on the plate in front of him then asked for three more helpings of kielbasa, sauerkraut, and boiled potatoes before barfing down two large slices of ginger cake for dessert. That was enough. He got up from the table, surging with energy. Adok looked around the room in search of something to climb up on, a ladder, a tall bookcase--anything.

Back home, Adok climbed trees. Adok loved scaling trees the way other boys loved sports. Soccer and hockey were the sports most boys played in his hometown. Soccer was fun, but it didn't excite Adok the way ascending a tall tree did. Climbing made Adok feel like he was journeying to an unknown world. He wasn't afraid of heights. The higher off the ground he got, the more thrilling it became. He could look down from the top and see the whole world and everybody in it. He would climb twenty-four hours a day if his parents allowed him. Adok instinctively knew which branches would support his weight and from which side of the tree was the easiest to ascend. He liked climbing most at night when the stars were out, and the moon was full. Then, his journey was to outer space.

That day, the day he was kidnapped and taken to a Lebensborn home, he climbed a pine tree in the wooded area of Waldorff's Park, where his family liked to picnic on Saturdays. It was a hot summer day on July 8, 1943. Adok heard his Mother calling him to lunch. She called him several times before his father joined in, threatening to get after him with a strap. They didn't see him, but Adok saw them. He was just two yards away, high in the sky, nestled between thick branches, wearing a beige, short-sleeve, cotton shirt and Khaki, wintergreen shorts with olive green knee-high socks. His parents and three-year-old brother, Arie, were reclining on a blanket on the grass.

Adok descended the tree and hopped down from the last branch nearest the ground. He was running when he tripped and fell. Just as he stood up, someone grabbed him from behind and put their hand over his mouth. He struggled but couldn't break free. He heard a click and saw the shiny steel blade of a knife. It was a short pocket knife with a pointed, jagged tip.

"Schreien Sie nicht, oder ich werde Ihren Hals schneiden."

The voice was gruff but feminine. The woman hissed, "Don't scream, or I'll cut your throat."

Adok looked up for the first time and saw the stern, rigid face of a German woman staring down at him with icy blue eyes and a surly demeanor. The top half of her left ear was missing. The woman wore a loose gray dress with black stockings and black lace-up shoes. She wore her blonde hair with white streaks in a ball at the nape of her neck. The woman looked to be the same age as Adok's Mother. She held the knife an inch from his face and turned the blade from right to left, then left to right. Adok stopped struggling and stood still, still enough to hear himself breathe. Tears streamed down his cheeks, but he didn't make a sound. Then from behind, another woman taped his mouth. That woman also tied his hands behind his back. Adok felt a sharp pain in his arm. After that, everything went black.

When Adok regained consciousness, he was lying on a cot in a large room with no windows. He felt a slight aching in his arm and lifted his head and looked about the long room. Ten cots were lining the wall on both sides, with his bed being the last one farthest from the door against the south wall. Boys his age and older occupied each bed. Several boys were sitting up. A couple glanced over at him. The look in their eyes was void of expression. Their faces were glum. Neither of them uttered a word.

The only light was from a single bulb hanging from a long cord dangling from the ceiling. The walls were dingy white with peeling plaster. The room was hot. Adok wondered what time it was if it was day or night. He wondered what his parents were doing, if they were searching for him; if his little brother was asking for him. Had they notified the police? Did their friends and neighbors, like Mr. Polanski, know he was missing?

"Have they tested you yet?"

Suddenly, Adok was aware of the clump of blonde hair and a pair of blue eyes peeking out from underneath the sheet in the bed next to him. The boy sat up all the way. Adok did too.

"If you don't pass, they send you to a concentration camp," the boy whispered. The boy's hair was disheveled. He wore a wrinkled, ratty t-shirt that was too small for him. Adok noticed a square piece of white cardboard posted to the wall above the boy's bed. Printed in big, black bold letters was the name Casmir. He then noticed that all the beds had the names of the boys posted above them. Adok looked on the wall behind him. A piece of cardboard hung over his bed too.

How do they know my name? The boy sat up all the way. Adok did too.

"How old are you, Adok?" Adok didn't answer. "I'm eight," said Casmir.

So am I, but I will not tell you.

"What's the test for?" Adok asked.

"To make sure you're pure and not a Jew or some other mixed race. You have to be pure Aryan. Look at us. We all have the same features. You must have blonde hair and blue eyes. There's no way you can be pure if you don't."

"Then why do we need to be tested since we all do?"

"Like I said, to make sure. There are Jews who dye their hair blonde, you know."

"Yes, I know," said Adok in a low voice. He immediately thought of Mrs. Steinberg, who used to live next door. She and her husband were Jews. Her hair was blonde. Adok never saw hair as beautiful as Mrs. Steinberg's. It was long, thick, and wavy. Even his mother thought so. His Mother often said Mrs. Steinberg's hair was shiny and looked like spun silk. But one day last summer, Mrs. Steinberg walked into his parent's butcher shop with black hair. Mother said she was made to dye it. Although Mrs. Steinberg protested, she was born with blonde hair. The German Consulate said a Jew couldn't be naturally blonde. The German Consulate gave Mrs. Steinberg a choice, either she dyes it, or they shave it.

My Mother, Arie, and I have blonde hair; my father's hair is black.

There were other laws and restrictions placed on Jews. Adok remembered his parents talking about how Jews couldn't travel by train without special permission. They had to wear the Star of David on their clothing. The law also prohibited Jews from leaving their homes between nine o'clock at night and five o'clock in the morning. Adok recalled how distraught the Steinberg's were when their synagogue was burned down. Even Adok's father, who considered Hitler, a great leader, was upset about it.

"No man has the right to desecrate another man's place of worship," his father said.

That same day, Mr. Steinberg came into the store and apologized to his father for not paying his butcher bill. The reason, Mr. Steinberg explained, was because all bank accounts owned by Jews were frozen, and he could withdraw only fifty dollars per week. Three days after Mrs. Steinberg dyed her hair, the two were sent to Krakow to live with other Jews.

"I was riding my scooter on the sidewalk in front of my house when they took me," said Casmir, out of the blue. "Minutes earlier, my Mother yelled down to me from my bedroom window, telling me that it was getting late and to come inside at once. It was the second time she called me. It was summertime and only six o'clock. It was still light outside, so I didn't want to come in just yet.

"Okay, I said. Then, I went speeding down the street for one last ride. When I got to the end of the street and stopped, suddenly a black car pulled up. The back door flung open. All I remember seeing was a pair of long, thin fingers reaching out and grabbing me by the neck so tightly that I could barely breathe. Then another hand grabbed hold of my arm and pulled me inside. It happened so fast. Just like that," said Casmir, popping his finger.

He shook his head. "If only I'd gone inside when my mother called me the first time."

If only I hadn't climbed that tree that day, Adok thought. Adok and Casmir sat in a quiet stupor for several minutes, just staring at the floor. A loud bong suddenly blasted through the walls, followed by an equally loud buzzing noise. Startled, Adok looked up. In the corner above his head was a black speaker box. The irritating buzzing continued. As soon as the bong sounded, all the boys jumped up and scurried out the door. A few fell trying to make it.

"You better hurry up or there won't be anything left," said Casmir. Casmir also hopped up. In a blink, he was out the door.

Adok followed, but a boy on the opposite side of the room screamed. The skinny kid reminded him of his brother, Arie. Adok went over to help. But the boy got up on his own before Adok could reach him. He shot past Adok and made it out the door just as it was closing. Adok hurried towards the exit. By then, the buzzing stopped. The door had closed. Adok went to open it, twisting and turning the knob several times, one way, and then the other. He pulled on the knob again and again, but it wouldn't budge. Frantically, Adok banged his fists on the door.

"Open up! Please. Somebody, let me out!" He banged as hard as he could until his hands hurt.

"Casmir!" Adok called. Adok soon realized that no one was coming. So Adok went back to his cot, laid down, and cried.

Two hours later, the boys returned. They filed in one-by-one, smiling now their bellies were full.

"You didn't make it did you?"

Adok shook his head. He was lying down with his hands under his head and his legs crossed, staring at the ceiling. His eyes were red, and his stomach was growling.

"Don't worry, tomorrow you'll eat. Everyone has been locked out of a meal at least once. So you have to be quick. You can't worry about others. It's everyone for himself when mealtime comes. You'll get the hang of it."

Adok didn't respond. He didn't want to get the hang of it. Whatever day or time of day it was, he wanted it to be over. He wished he was home in his bed with his own family. He didn't understand why he was here. He had done nothing wrong. He wasn't a Jew. Adok closed his eyes and prayed that he would wake up tomorrow and discover this was all a bad dream.

The next morning, the bong sounded. Adok jumped out of bed and raced to the door. He didn't even bother to put on his shoes. He was still wearing the beige shirt and wintergreen shorts he had worn the day he had been kidnapped. The buzzing noise was still ringing in his ears when he entered the cafeteria. He found the right room by following the smell. He was the first one in line.

Several women wearing red aprons with white ruffled fringe were standing behind a long table, ready to serve. On the table were trays filled with sausage, egg croquettes, toast, marmalade, slices of Gouda cheese, fresh fruit, and pitchers of milk. Adok smiled at all the food. He was so hungry that he could taste the bratwurst in his mouth already. Today he would eat. He looked behind him to see where Casmir was. There was no one there. None of the other boys were in line.

"You must wash and recite the morning pledge in the assembly hall before breakfast," said a large woman with a scruffy voice. She was the first woman standing behind the table. She raised her arm and pointed to the doorway. Adok's heart sank, and he suddenly felt faint. He dropped his head into his chest and turned to leave, but a girl stopped him. The girl was also wearing a red apron. She approached him with a wet washcloth and washed his face and hands. Alenka had the face of an angel with rosy-pink cheeks, crystal blue eyes, and light blonde, shoulder-length hair. She looked to be a teenager. Adok couldn't help but notice the bulge in her blouse. He guessed she had to be at least thirteen or fourteen.

"You're the boy who arrived two days ago, aren't you?" she asked, kneeling in front of him.

Adok nodded, "I guess so."

"He must go to the assembly hall," repeated the large woman.

The girl looked at her.

"Please, Fraulein Helga, let him eat. You see how hungry he is. He's just a little boy. Just let him eat. You don't have to worry. I'll tell Fraulein Hess. You won't have to say anything. I'll take the blame."

"You may take the blame, but I'll get the punishment," growled Fraulein Helga.

The girl grabbed a plate and filled it with double portions of everything on the table. Helga poured a glass of milk and handed it to Adok.

"Here, take him in the pantry out of sight before she comes looking for him."

Adok followed the girl into the kitchen. She opened the door to the pantry and then closed it.

"No, out in the shed is better."

The girl led Adok out the back door, across a patch of grass, and through a gate to the shed.

"In here." She clicked on the light. "Now stay here and eat. Hurry up, but don't eat too fast, or you'll get sick. When done, hide the plate and glass in one of these crates. I'll get it later. I'll lock the gate, so you'll have to climb the wall to get back. Fraulein Hess will punish you, but she was going to punish you anyway for being late to the assembly. Now, at least it will be on a full stomach."

The girl opened the door and then turned around before leaving. "By the way, my name is Alenka," she said, flashing a dimpled smile.

Adok immediately smiled back. That was his Mother's name. Adok ate, but not too fast. He ate everything on his plate and then did just as Alenka told him. He hid the dishes in the crate he was sitting on and then hurried out of the shed. He climbed the wall and ran across the grass and through the back door. He was about to enter the kitchen when he noticed an open door at the end of a long dark hallway to his left. He went that way instead. Slowly, but quietly, he crept towards the doorway.

Sunlight filled the room. When Adok reached the door, he suddenly stood in the assembly hall. It was as large as an auditorium. Four round Greek columns, reaching from the floor to the ceiling, divided the room into three large sections. The children sat in the middle section between four evenly-spaced columns with their backs to him. They sat in rows of foldable wooden chairs, ten chairs in a row.

There were six rows of chairs on one side, separated by a wide aisle, and six rows on the other side. The girls sat on the far side opposite four large windows to the right--the boys on the left side. The boys occupied only the first four rows of seats. All the chairs on the girl's side were full. All the boys dressed alike in light brown, long-sleeved shirts and black ties, dark brown knickers, matching knee-high socks, and black lace-up shoes.

The girls wore white short-sleeved blouses, baby blue neckerchiefs, and navy blue pleated skirts, with white ankle socks and black and white loafers.

Three tall blonde women dressed in military uniforms stood in front of the assembly behind a long desk. Each wore a gray skirt and a double-breasted jacket with a black tie. Pinned on the tie was a circular metal brooch of black enamel trimmed in yellow with a yellow blitz motif in the center. Woven into the button-down flap on the right breast pocket of each jacket was a black swastika with white trim. Adok recognized the tallest woman in the middle. She also wore an Iron Cross pinned to her left breast pocket and a gun holster. She was the same woman that held the knife to his face.

That must be Fraulein Hess. Fraulein Hess was looking down at some papers on the desk while the other two women watched the children. No one heard Adok enter. Adok could feel the tension in the room as all the children looked too scared to do anything but sit up straight in their seats with their hands pinned to their sides, and their eyes focused directly in front. Adok walked across the highly-polished floor towards the assembly, praying no one would see him. Don't be afraid. Just walk over to one of the empty rows and sit down. If asked why you're late, tell the truth. How can they punish you for not knowing what to do? If they do punish you, so be it. As Alenka said, you already ate.

"Alenka Kaminski," Fraulein Hess called out.

The loud and sudden sound of her gruff voice startled everyone, including the other frauleins. Adok froze in place in mid-step. He looked at Fraulein Hess as did everyone else. Fraulein Hess was looking to her left on the girl's side of the room. Adok dropped to his knees and quickly crawled several feet across the remaining distance to the empty chairs behind the second row on the boy's side. He made his way to the far end, to the last chair near the center aisle, before he quietly rose just high enough to slide his butt into the seat. No one saw him. Everyone's eyes were on Alenka walking across the room in front of the girls in the first row. Alenka stopped in the center aisle, turned, and faced the frauleins. She was no longer wearing her apron but the same uniform as the other girls.

Fraulein Hess clasped her hands behind her back and glared down her thin pencil nose at Alenka.

"Recite the oath."

Adok watched as Alenka straightened her shoulders and stiffened her back. She pressed her left arm against the side of her body and then raised her right hand. With an open palm, Alenka began:

"I swear a solemn oath to the savior of our country, Adolf Hitler. I am willing and ready to give up my life for him, so help me God."

Fraulein Hess nodded, and Alenka returned to her seat.

Adok couldn't see Alenka's face but could tell she was happy and relieved by the way she swung her arms as she walked.

Fraulein Hess paused again. She gazed down at the papers on the desk before suddenly lifting her eyes without raising her head. She flashed Adok a hard stare. Adok immediately felt a chill creep down his spine. He gasped as did most of the other children. Some turned their heads to see who had caught the mean fraulein's attention. Fraulein Hess said nothing. She just lowered her eyes again. One, two, three minutes passed. The hall was deathly still. No one spoke a syllable or moved a muscle. The wait had the intended effect of making everyone nervous, wondering who would be the fraulein's next victim.

She saw me all along. What if she calls me? She's going to call me next. I must remember the oath. "To the savior of our country, Adolf Hitler. I am willing…"

"Casmir Pawlak!"

Adok stopped trying to recall the oath and watched Casmir make his way to the center aisle. Casmir was trembling and looked terrified. The front section of his hair was standing straight up. Casmir raised his right hand and began: "To the Fuhrer of our country, I'm willing and able to sacrifice my life, so help me God."

Immediately, Fraulein Hess motioned with her hand across her throat. Casmir shrieked. Boom! Fraulein Hess stomped her foot. Everyone jumped. The sound vibrated across the floor. Casmir froze and stood as still as a wooden post. Though Casmir's back was to him, Adok could tell he wasn't breathing.

Suddenly Casmir collapsed. He was now lying in the aisle, curled up unconscious. Everyone remained silent. None of the children looked at Casmir. No one tried to help him.

"Adok Makowski!" The voice of Fraulein Hess sounded even louder and harsher than before.

Adok jumped out of his chair and rushed to the front. He stepped over Casmir without looking down. Raising his right hand, Adok stood with his feet together, his shoulders back, and his chest out. The way he had seen German soldiers stationed in his hometown stand at attention.

"I swear a solemn oath to the savior of our country, Adolf Hitler. I am willing…"

Adok paused. He forgot what came next. Closing his eyes, he tried to recall Alenka's exact words.

"When you want to remember something, you've heard, picture the words in your mind," his teacher and neighbor Mr. Polanski told him. "I am willing…" No, start from the beginning. Adok took a deep breath and began again. His eyes remained closed.

"I swear a solemn oath to the savior of our country, Adolf Hitler. I-I am willing and ready to give up my life for him, so help me God."

Slowly, Adok opened his eyes. Fraulein Hess squinted then nodded at him. "That is correct."

Her words were quick and sharp. Adok exhaled but was too afraid to move. Fraulein Hess nodded again. This time Adok turned around. He automatically looked down. Casmir was no longer lying on the floor. He wondered where Casmir was. Adok returned to his seat and noticed that one fraulein was missing.

Fraulein Hess finally dismissed the assembly, but no one dared to leave. Walking down the center aisle, Fraulein Hess took long, deliberate strides. She looked ten feet tall as she passed. She was as intimidating as any male soldier Adok had seen in the German Army. All the children stood at attention in front of their chairs. Only when the door closed did the children draw breath. Everyone sighed and hurried to the cafeteria. Adok followed Alenka back down the long dark hallway to the kitchen. "Aren't you going to eat breakfast?" Adok asked.

"I already ate. Since I help out in the kitchen, I get to eat first. It means I have to wake up at five o'clock in the morning, but it's worth it because I never miss a meal."

"What's going to happen to Casmir? Will he be all right?"

"I don't know. But he'll miss breakfast and maybe lunch, and dinner too. It all depends on how many demerits he gets and how many points he has accumulated. You must earn everything you get, and everything you do either adds or takes away points. It takes a total of seventy-five points to eat breakfast, lunch, and dinner. That's twenty-five points per meal. When you first arrive, every child gets seventy-five points to start, but that's just for one day. If you want to eat the next day, you must earn more points."

"How many points do you get from reciting the oath correctly?"

"Everything is worth twenty-five points, but you can earn extra points for taking the initiative and doing things better or faster than anyone else. Like this morning, you recited the oath after only hearing it once. So you'll get fifty points--twenty-five for reciting the oath correctly and another twenty-five for doing it on your first try. That usually doesn't happen. I was the only other person that was able to recite the oath correctly, word-for-word, on the very first time like you."

Adok watched a wide grin grow on Alenka's face as the two entered the kitchen.

"Sit here, I have to make the bread for lunch," she said, pointing to the long table in the center of the room. Adok sat down as Alenka grabbed a large mixing bowl, a bag of flour, yeast, and other ingredients from the cabinets and placed them on the table. She stood across from him on the opposite side and poured the ingredients into the bowl.

"Will I get points taken away for being late to the assembly?"

"Well, not this time. That's because Fraulein Helga interceded on your behalf to Fraulein Hess. They're sisters, you know. Fraulein Helga is five years older. She's the only person who can talk Fraulein Hess out of things, her and Fraulein Franziska."

"If Fraulein Helga is older than her sister, why isn't she in charge?"

Did you notice the Iron Cross Fraulein Hess wears on her uniform? It's one of the highest medals you can get in the German Army. She was awarded it for shooting down fifty enemy planes in one night, and that was after she was wounded. She served in the women's air force auxiliary in the anti-aircraft unit. She would still be in service today if a bullet hadn't blown off part of her ear. Helga has been a cook all her life and was deemed physically unfit to join because of her weight."

"What about the test to determine if I'm of pure blood? Casmir says if I don't pass, I'll get sent to a concentration camp."

Alenka frowned. "Yes, that's true. Though, you'll be rewarded one hundred points if you are of Nordic blood. It's the only time you can earn that many points for one thing."

"But if you're blonde with blue eyes, how can anyone tell just by looking at you that you're not Aryan?"

"Fraulein Franziska performs the test. According to Franziska, the specifications of a true Aryan are tall with a long head, a narrow face, a well-defined chin, a straight nose with a very high root--whatever that means--soft golden blonde hair, light blue or gray eyes, and a pink-white skin."

"Wow!" Adok touched his nose and chin. "Do I have all those features?"

"Yes, as far as I can tell. But I'm not an expert." "When do you think I'll get tested?"

Suddenly, Alenka froze and didn't answer. Adok could feel the hot breath of someone breathing on the back of his neck. But he was too afraid to turn around and see who it was. Clap! Adok winced. Without moving his head, Adok peeked out of the corner of his eye and saw a hand with long, thin fingers clutching his shoulder so tightly he couldn't move.

"Adok Makowski! Come with me!"

CHAPTER NINE

Unknown German School Teacher, 1932

Fraulein Franziska was one of the two women dressed in military garb standing beside Fraulein Hess during the morning assembly. Now, she was wearing a nurse's uniform complete with a white cap. Like Fraulein Hess, she combed her blonde hair back and pinned it into a ball. The blue and white striped, long-sleeved seersucker dress she wore had a white round collar and was buttoned in the front. Over it was a starched white, body-length apron that tied in the back. Adok followed Fraulein Franziska to the basement.

They walked through the ten-bed infirmary to a room at the far end. All ten beds lined the east wall. Against the opposite wall was a gray metal desk with a lamp sitting on it, flanked by two, lumpy green sofas. At first, Adok saw no one in the beds as he walked by. All the beds had clean white pillowcases and folded-down top sheets. Then out of the corner of his eye, he spotted a clump of blonde hair sticking out from underneath the sheet in the last bed before he entered the room.

Casmir!

Adok wanted to go to him but dared not. He entered the pale blue room instead. It reeked of rubbing alcohol. Adok held his breath for a while until he no longer felt the urge to sneeze. Positioned against the farthest wall was a high-standing examination bed directly below a narrow window. Cater-corner to the bed, on the left-hand side, was a white wooden desk and chair. A long white step-on scale measuring both height and weight occupied the opposite wall across from the table. Fraulein Franziska sat down. Adok stood on the other side of the desk, facing her. Numerous large and small pictures of different facial shapes hung on the wall behind her, including enlarged photographs of eyes, ears, noses, chins, lips, and foreheads. The images were divided into two groups. On the right side, a plaque above them read: "Characteristics of Pure Nordic Ancestry."

On the left side, the plaque read: "Traits of Jewish Anti-humans."

"What is your name?"

Fraulein Franziska had a robust and commanding voice like Fraulein Hess but with less edge.

"Adok Makowski," said Adok, without emotion. "Your full name is Adok Bohdan Makowski.

You were born on April 9, 1936, to Bartek and Alenka Makowski. Your mother's maiden name is Cebulski. You have a three-year-old brother named Arie Adolf. They live at 68 Bukowa Street in Slupsk. Your father is a butcher and owns a store."

Adok slowly nodded his head, wondering how she knew so much about him.

"I guess you're wondering how I know all of this?" asked Fraulein Franziska, smiling. She didn't wait for Adok to answer.

"Your parents told us when they signed the papers giving you up for adoption. You see, your parents want you to become a German citizen. They want you to have the best in life, and they realize a German family can give you what they can't. Your father is a great admirer of Hitler, is he not? He was very excited about the whole thing. Of course, they were worried that you wouldn't understand. So, they thought it best that we take you at a time and place of our choosing. That was the easy part. Now is the test. Do you know why you're here?" Fraulein Franziska asked in a stern voice.

"Yes-I-yes," Adok nodded timidly, still thinking about what she said about his parents giving him away. He could feel himself about to cry. Tears creased the corner of his eyes. He blinked several times, forcing them back.

"What's that? Speak up. Nordic children are not weak and whiny; they are strong and active, particularly the boys."

Remember, anyone who doesn't pass the test is sent to a concentration camp, to a concentration camp, a concentration camp.

"Yes, Fraulein Franziska, I know why I am here. I'm here for a noble purpose, to determine if I am of Pure Nordic blood. I am not afraid. I welcome such examination, for I know that I am. And I am honored that I was selected to-to…."

Adok shouted the words and spoke them with such fire and conviction that Fraulein Franziska sprung to her feet. Leaning over her desk, the Fraulein peered directly into Adok's eyes.

"To create an Order of good blood that can serve Germany and commit itself without sparing itself," she recited. "To create an Order of good blood that will so spread the idea of Nordic blood that we shall attract to us all the Nordic blood in the world, and thus, create a master race of Aryan superhumans," she completed.

Fraulein Franziska straightened her posture. "Is that what you wanted to say, Herr Adok?"

"Yes, Fraulein!" he proclaimed, shaking his head up and down vigorously. He felt overwhelmed to the point of dizziness and leaned against the desk to keep from falling. Still looking directly into his eyes, Fraulein Franziska continued: "In America, their Constitution states that all men are created equal and that such equality is self-evident and bestowed upon men by their Creator."

"What nonsense! All men are not equal. Nor did God intend them to be. The worldview of Germany is that human inequality is obvious among the various races of people, among red and yellow people, and particularly among the Negroes. That whites are superior to them all is evident. But not all whites are the same either. The term Caucasian is used loosely to denote all people with white skin pigment. But merely having white skin doesn't mean your bloodline is pure. Do you understand what I am saying?"

First, Adok shook his head from side-to-side and quickly nodded up and down. Fraulein Franziska turned and gestured to the photographs behind her.

"To the careful observer, differences in physical features--the size and shape of the head, nose, mouth, et cetera--can be found among Caucasians. The color of the eyes, hair, and skin also varies, which is why purity tests are essential."

Adok's pulse raced when Fraulein Franziska stepped around the desk and walked over to the examination table. "Remove all your clothes and step up onto the bed."

Adok obeyed and stripped down to his socks. He stepped forward with his hands covering his private parts. Immediately, Fraulein Franziska picked him up and sat him on the examination bed. He shivered. The sheet on the bed was cold against his bare bottom.

Reaching into her apron pocket, she pulled out a large round magnifying glass and proceeded to examine Adok's hair and scalp. She then measured his chest and the length of his arms. She weighed Adok on a large scale and measured his hips. After that, Fraulein Franziska photographed Adok's face and head from every angle.

Three hours later, Adok entered the cafeteria for lunch dressed like the other boys. Having showered, he looked fresh, pressed, and clean. Like his fellow Nordic brethren, his hair was combed long on the top and cut short in the back and on the sides--Hitler Youth style. Fraulein Helga smiled and winked at him when he approached the serving table and took a plate. All the other children were already seated and eating lunch, the boys on one side of the cafeteria and the girls on the other.

"I see it went well," said Alenka, emerging from the kitchen carrying a pitcher of milk. She set the pitcher down on the table. "You must have passed, or you wouldn't be dressed like that."

Adok just grinned and filled his plate. He was about to sit down at a table with the other boys when Alenka grabbed his arm.

"No, come with me."

He followed her through the kitchen and out the back door to the same small grassy area he had crossed earlier that day. This time, they sat on the round wooden table under the only tree in the courtyard.

"Here." Alenka pulled a piece of paper from her apron pocket and handed it to Adok.

"It's a copy of the five oaths we have to remember in case Fraulein Hess calls on you again. Just because you recited one correctly today, doesn't mean you'll be able to do so tomorrow. The best way to remember them all is to read them over two or three times every night before you go to bed and at least once or twice in the morning before the bong. Remember, everything you do, except eating, can earn you points or demerits. Demerits take away whatever points you have. One demerit equals ten points. You currently have accumulated one hundred and fifty points so far, but let's say that later this afternoon, for some reason, you receive five demerits, that's fifty points subtracted from your total."

"What's going to happen later this afternoon?"

"Physical training classes, every morning, boys march and perform military drills. You have to learn how to march in formation behind the drill leader and follow his commands. You are given a long wooden baton to march with at first until you learn the drills and can walk without dropping the stick. Then you are given a rifle. Some of the boys are chosen to be color bearers and carry flag poles. The drill leaders all carry thin, metal swords."

"You mean we get real swords and rifles?"

"Yes, of course, only the rifles aren't loaded, and the blades on the swords are very dull."

"Do the girls drill too?"

"Yes, but only for fifteen minutes. We do domestic work for the rest of the morning. Some of us are assigned to mop floors and clean windows, some to do laundry, and some to do gardening. But in the afternoon, we all go to gymnastics and physical training classes."

"What about school?"

"We have school every day for an hour following lunch. It's not anything like the school in Poland. There are no bulky textbooks on subjects like science, history, or geography. We don't learn much about what you call traditional education. Math is the only real subject we study. Instead, we receive pamphlets recounting the life of the Fuhrer or books on the Jews. For the boys, the focus is mainly on learning how to be a good soldier.

The focus of the girls is on learning how to be good mothers and wives. Whatever materials you get, memorize and learn them quickly. That's the key to earning points for schoolwork. How well you perform and obey is how you win points for everything else. You must think of everything you do and say as a test. Even when the frauleins are not present, words have a way of getting back to them about something you may have said, or did, so be careful. Now hurry up and eat. You don't want to be late to class, that's two demerits."

Adok followed Alenka to class. All the classrooms were on the second floor. The cafeteria and boy's dormitory were on the first floor. The girl's dormitory was on the third.

"There's the boy's classroom for your age," said Alenka, pointing to the room across the hall from the one she was about to enter.

Adok hesitated. He felt safe with Alenka and didn't want to leave her. She was the only friend he had and the only other person he knew besides Casmir.

"Don't worry; you'll be alright. Go on now, before your teacher comes."

Reluctantly Adok walked across the hall. It was a bright, sunny room with six windows, three facing west and three in the back of the room facing north. Behind the teacher's desk was a black chalkboard. There were four rows of chairs with six chairs in a row. Everyone had designated seats. A white piece of paper with Adok's name printed on it was taped to the back of the chair on the first desk in the last row by the window. The light brown, oak wood desks were identical to the ones at his school in Poland.

The desk behind him had Casmir's name on it. It was empty. As soon as Adok sat down, the teacher, walking fast, entered the room. She was tall and slender. Her long blonde hair was pinned up in a ponytail that swooshed when she walked. Black-rim glasses covered her light gray eyes. Like all the frauleins, she wore a gray military uniform. But her small waistline made the suit look more flattering on her figure than on the other frauleins.

"Good afternoon, class."

"Good afternoon, Fraulein Serena." All the boys greeted her in unison.

"Take out your books, please." Adok watched the other boys lift their desktops and retrieve two books. There were only two inside the desk. He did the same. The name of the first book was The Poisonous Mushroom, by Julius Streicher. It was green with yellow handwriting in German. The picture on the cover was of five mushrooms. The mushrooms had human faces depicted on the top half of the stem underneath the dome-shaped caps. The middle mushroom was the largest. The face on the stem was of a man with enormous sad eyes and a big, long nose. On the bottom half of its stem was the Star of David. The second book was titled Trust No Fox on His Green Heath and No Jew on His Oath by Elvira Bauer and published by Julius Streicher. The red book had white handwriting in German. In the upper right-hand corner was a circle with a profile of a balding, grouchy, humped-back Jewish man with a big nose holding up two fingers. Above his head was the Star of David. In the lower left-hand corner was a circle with a picture of a sinister-looking brown fox lurking in the grass.

"Everyone, please open the book, The Poisonous Mushroom," instructed Fraulein Serena.

"Jerard Kaczmarek, begin reading."

Jerard rose and stood beside his desk. He was the third boy in the row next to Adok. He was stocky with a thick neck and plump cheeks. He wasn't fat, though. He was solid. He opened to the first page and read: "A Mother and her young boy are gathering mushrooms in the German forest. The boy finds some poisonous ones. The Mother explains that there are good mushrooms and poisonous ones, and, as they go home, says: "Look, Franz, human beings in this world are like the mushrooms in the forest. There are good mushrooms, and there are good people. There are poisonous, bad mushrooms, and there are bad people. And we must be on our guard against bad people just as we have to be on guard against poisonous mushrooms. Do you understand that?"

"Yes, Mother," Franz replies. "I understand that in dealing with bad people, trouble may arise, just as when one eats a poisonous mushroom. One may even die!"

"And do you know, too, who these bad men are, these poisonous mushrooms of mankind?" the mother continued. "Franz slaps his chest in pride: "Of course, I know, Mother! They are the Jews! Our teacher has often told us about them." "The Mother praises her boy for his intelligence and goes on to explain the different kinds of "poisonous" Jews: the Jewish peddler, the Jewish cattle dealer, the Kosher butcher, the Jewish doctor, the baptized Jew, and so on."

"However they disguise themselves, or however, friendly they try to be, affirming a thousand times their good intentions to us, one must not believe them. Jews they are and Jews they remain. For our Volk, they are poison."

"Like the poisonous mushroom!" says Franz. "Yes, my child! Just as a single poisonous mushroom can kill a whole family, so a solitary Jew can destroy a whole village, a whole city, even an entire Volk."

"Franz has understood."

"Tell me, Mother, do all non-Jews know that the Jew is as dangerous as a poisonous mushroom?"

"Mother shakes her head." Adok felt uneasy as he read along and didn't want to listen anymore. He thought about the Steinberg's. They weren't poisonous mushrooms. They were good people, kind and hardworking, just like his parents. They always gave him a gift on his birthday. He liked to collect spinning tops, and whenever the Steinberg's came across a unique one, they bought it for him. He had over twenty spinning tops back home. It's a lie. It's all a lie. It's not the Jews that stole me away from my parents. No, that's you, Fraulein Hess. It's not the Steinberg's claiming that my parents gave me away and didn't want me anymore. No, that's you, Fraulein Franziska. It's not the other races of people that want to dominate everyone else and are waging war with the whole world. No, that's you, Hitler and Germany. Adok slammed closed the book. He glanced up at the teacher. She was looking down at her desk. He sighed;

thankful she hadn't seen him. He looked around the room. Everyone else had also closed the first book. They were now opening the second.

"For fifty points, who wants to be the first to recite from memory the first two paragraphs of the book, Trust no Fox?"

Everyone's hands shot up except Adok's. Fraulein Serena scanned the room and then called on Damian Dudek. Damian stood and began:

"At the creation of the world, the Lord God conceived the races: Red Indians, Negroes, and Chinese, and Jew, too, the rotten crew. And we were also on the scene: We Germans midst this motley medley. He gave them all a piece of earth to work with the sweat of their brow. But the Jew went on strike at once! For the devil rode him from the first. Cheating, not working was his aim; for lying, he got first prize in less than no time from the Father of Lies. Then he wrote it in the Talmud. By the banks of Pharaoh's Nile, Pharaoh saw this folk and said: "I'll torment the lazy blighters; these people shall make bricks for me.""

"The Jew did this all wailing and whining, never was there such cursing and swearing, with bent backs and over-big slippers. Even today, we see them shambling, with lips hanging down and great red noses and looking daggers, flashing hate. They owe the pharaoh thanks, who trounced them soundly for their pranks. The Jews soon had enough of that! The Devil brought them to Germany. Like thieves, they stole our land, hoping to get the upper hand." Fraulein

Serena clapped. The other students joined in. Adok didn't.

"Now for twenty-five points, who would like to recite the third paragraph? Hmm, let's see, Stanley Nowak."

Stanley spoke loud with inflection in his voice as he stood proudly with his chest out. He gestured with his hands, delivering a very animated recital. "But the Germans--they stand foursquare. Look, children, and the two compare, the German and the Jew. Take a good look at the two in the picture drawn for you. A joke--you think it is only that? Easy to guess which is which, I say: The German is a proud young man, able to work and able to fight. Because he is a fine big chap, for danger he does not care a rap, the Jew has always hated him! Here is the Jew, as all can see, biggest ruffian in our country; He thinks himself the greatest beau, and yet is the ugliest, you know!"

Once again, everyone clapped. The teacher gave Stanley an extra twenty-five points for his lively address. She was about to enlist another to recite the fourth paragraph when the bell rang. The Class was over. Physical training was next. Adok was happy. He was the first to jump out of his chair and head for the door.

"Adok Makowski, not so fast, young man. Come here!" The teacher's voice had changed from friendly to stern. Adok stopped and turned around. His heart quickened.

Fraulein Serena walked up to him.

"Show me your hands," demanded Fraulein Serena.

Adok obeyed, holding out both palms for her to see.

She grabbed both his hands and scrutinized his palms, then turned them over and checked the back of his hands before letting go.

"Do you know why I asked to see your hands?" Adok shook his head.

"No fraulein."

"Because I noticed that you didn't clap after any of your classmate's recitals. I wondered if your hands were injured. But I see they are not. So tomorrow, I expect to see you clapping like the other children. If you know what's good for you."

Adok nodded before bursting into tears. "I just want to go home. I want my mother! I don't hate Jewish people. I don't hate anybody. Please, please, fraulein, just let me go home." He continued crying as he hung his head down.

"Adok, Adok!" Fraulein Serena bent over and lifted his chin to her eyes. "Look at me, son. Germany is your home now. You must accept that. I know it's hard. I'm not without sympathy, like some. But tears will do you no good here. You must be strong and determined to survive at all costs, which means that even if you don't hate the Jews, you must pretend like you do and talk like you do. If you don't, you may share their fate. You don't want that, do you? You don't want to go to a concentration camp? You don't want to die, do you?"

"No, fraulein, I don't want to die."

"Then pretend, just pretend. You must learn how to be a good actor, Adok, like so many of us have. Your previous life no longer exists, including your family, and everything you once believed in, you must now forget. So dry your eyes and hurry to the gymnasium. You still have enough time to change. Go quickly!"

Adok ran out of the room and down the four flights of stairs. At the bottom of the last flight, Alenka was waiting for him. "What happened to you? I was getting worried. Here," she said, handing him a white t-shirt, black shorts, white socks, and a pair of black sneakers, with white rubber soles.

"There are lockers in the boy's restroom. Go and change and hurry up! The frauleins will be down in a few minutes."

Adok obeyed.

The gymnasium was in the basement, down the hall from the infirmary. Various gymnastic apparatus was set up around the gym. In the center of the gym were two large black square mats arranged side by side on the floor. The boys sat on one mat, the girls on the other. Everyone dressed alike.

Adok and Alenka came in and sat down across from each other on separate mats behind the other children. It was the first time Adok noticed the other children's reaction to Alenka when no adults were around. All stopped talking when she approached, like when a fraulein was present. But it wasn't out of fear or respect. By the frowns on their faces, no one liked Alenka. Some girls even turned their heads away as if disgusted by the sight of her. Others wouldn't look at her. The boys just stared stoically. One boy's stare stood out. Henryk was thirteen and the oldest boy at the Lebensborn Home. When he looked at

Alenka, Adok could only describe it as hate. Alenka tried to pretend she didn't notice. It was apparent by the change in her demeanor that their stares made her uncomfortable, especially Henryk's. She flashed, Henryk a faint smile before she sat down and quickly looked away.

Adok leaned over the side edge of the boy's mat. "Why does everyone look at you like they dislike you?"

"They're just jealous because I get a lot of privileges and they don't, that's all. Don't mind them." Adok was about to ask another question when the sound of a whistle brought everyone to their feet. Sixteen frauleins entered in single file led by Fraulein Hess and followed by Fraulein Franziska, then Fraulein Serena, and then Fraulein Helga. They were all wearing gray sweatsuits and white sneakers.

"Henryk Jablonski, what is Hitler's proclamation for German youth?" Fraulein Hess asked as she and the other frauleins marched by, between the two mats. "German youth of the future must be slim and slender, swift like the greyhound, tough like leather, and hard like Krupp steel," Henryk shouted. He was standing directly in front of Adok.

"Excellent, twenty-five points to you," said Fraulein Hess, now standing facing the class as was the other frauleins.

"I want each of you to go and stand by the apparatus you think you've mastered. You wait there until one of us comes over to test you. On some, your test will be on how well you perform. On others, speed will be the test."

Fraulein Hess blew her whistle, and everyone scattered. Adok knew precisely where to go. He had spotted two long ropes at the far end of the gym when he entered. They were hanging down from the ceiling crossbeams. Adok rushed over to the ropes. He tugged on one to see how sturdy and secure it was. He was surprised to look over and see Alenka tugging on the other.

"Don't look so surprised, Adok. Girls can climb too. My parents used to perform a high-wire act in the circus. They were very popular before the war. You may have heard of them. They called themselves The Great Kaminski's. I used to perform with them occasionally. I used to do flips in the air and everything. But what amazed the audience was how fast a skinny, nine-year-old girl could climb up a rope. I'd get a standing ovation every time I'd climbed."

Alenka gripped the rope with both hands. "Well, come on. Let's see who can reach the top first."

Adok had never competed against a girl before. He didn't even know if it was legal. "We have to wait for one of the frauleins," Adok said.

He noticed Alenka glance over her shoulder and smile. He followed her gaze. Fraulein Hess and the other Frauleins were standing behind him, and all the children around the gym were staring at them. Fraulein Hess put her whistle in her mouth and nodded.

"Ready?" said Alenka.

Adok turned and gripped the rope with both hands. Something told him that the only thing worse than competing against a girl was losing to a girl. Alenka was taller and older than he was and probably even stronger. But he had to beat her. He had to.

Fraulein Hess blew the whistle again. Adok hopped onto the rope. Right hand left hand--don't look at Alenka--right hand, left hand; don't look down, just look up--right hand, left hand, faster, faster, faster. Suddenly, Adok heard a thump and felt a sharp pain. He winced. He had bumped his head on a crossbeam. He didn't stop, though. He quickly scurried back down the rope, feeling dizzy as he went. He didn't know where Alenka was until he was two feet from the floor and jumped down. Only then did he rub the top of his head and look up. Alenka was just reaching the top. She looked down at him before descending. Adok discovered something else about Alenka that day. She didn't like to lose.

"I'm sorry," said Adok, reacting to the distraught look on Alenka's face once she had descended and was standing next to him. But there was more in her eyes than just disappointment. Adok didn't know how to describe it, but it frightened him.

"Seventy-five points to Adok," announced Fraulein Hess. Fraulein Hess then flashed Alenka a hard, disappointing gaze.

"Five demerits," she announced to Alenka in a cold, steely voice. Alenka gasped, put her hand over her mouth, and ran out of the gym.

Adok noticed the other children smiling at him when he walked back to the mat and sat down. He felt sad and uncertain about Alenka. One-by-one, the other kids completed their apparatus and joined him. The first was Henryk. Henryk sat next to Adok.

"Wow! That was great. I never saw anyone climb a rope so fast," said Henryk, whose specialty was performing gymnastics on the High bar.

"Don't feel bad for Alenka. It serves her right. It's her fault she got demerits. She challenged you. That's the rule. If you challenge someone, or someone challenges you, the winner automatically gets seventy-five points. The loser gets five demerits."

"So, if Alenka hadn't challenged me?"

"If she hadn't challenged you, the two of you would have been timed, and as long as she beat the clock, no matter how much faster you were, she would have gotten twenty-five points. You still would have gotten an extra twenty-five points for beating the clock so handily, but your total would have been only fifty, not seventy-five."

"Oh, I see. You and the other kids don't like Alenka, do you?"

"The rest of us don't challenge each other--ever. We don't want to gain points at the expense of one of us being forced to skip meals. It's not necessary. The frauleins ride us enough with their constant scrutinizing of everything we do and endless demands for us to memorize this and recite that. Alenka is so desperate for their approval that she's willing to do anything to get it. You can't trust her. Alenka is like a chameleon. One day she's your friend and all kindness and sweetness. The next day she's revealing your secrets to the frauleins and getting you into trouble. That's why no one likes her."

"Is that the only reason why you dislike her so much?" Adok watched as the look on Henryk's face turned even tauter.

"Yes, but that's because my younger sister, Ewa, was her first victim. Ewa and I were very close. We were only sixteen months apart in age. All three of us were brought here last year. We arrived on the same day, June 13, 1942. My sister and Alenka became best friends the moment they met. She was the older sister Ewa always wanted. I liked her too. I think all the children liked her at first. Though we were all afraid and upset about being taken from our parents, the circumstances that brought Alenka here were much more tragic.

My sister and I rode the school bus to school every day. We lived the farthest from school, so we were always the first kids to be picked up in the morning and the last ones to be dropped off in the afternoon. One day a new bus driver picked us up. Our regular bus driver was sick, the substitute said. We were driven to school that morning, as usual. But after school, the driver took all the other kids home. We were driven here instead.

The substitute bus driver was Fraulein Serena. Alenka never revealed to Ewa or me or anyone else how her abduction occurred. My sister slept in the bed next to her, and Ewa used to tell me about the awful nightmares Alenka had. We all felt sorry for her. But one day, six months ago, Alenka stopped having dreams, and everything changed. Alenka finally talked about her family and upbringing. She told Ewa about her family's circus act and how she used to perform on the high wire with her parents. That's when my sister told Alenka how afraid she was of heights. After that, Alenka challenged Ewa to climb the rope.

The rules demanded that my sister accept the challenge, even though she didn't want to. My sister would always lose. She would get mid-way and freeze. It got to where Alenka was challenging my sister every week. I begged Alenka to stop, and so did the other children, but she wouldn't. Every time my sister lost five, demerits went against her. She could no longer eat regularly. One week, Ewa didn't eat for six days straight. That's when Fraulein Helga and Serena talked Fraulein Hess and the others into changing the rules. Now you can only challenge someone twice a month.

The new regulations require that an entire seven days pass between challenges. The rule change finally allowed my sister to eat. But I knew Alenka would re-challenge her once the allotted time was up, so I made Ewa practice every day.

"Just close your eyes and work your way up the rope slowly," I told her.

"Pretend you're ascending to heaven," I said. On the last day of practice, Ewa finally got the hang of it and made it to the top and back down several times without freezing or slipping off. The next day was the challenge. Alenka was just a little bit ahead of her. Ewa made it to the top okay and was on her way down," said Henryk.

Then Henryk's voice cracked as his eyes filled with tears. "It happened so fast. She was scaling down and dropped. She was midway. There was a thump, a loud, hard thump. Her head hit--her eyes were open. She was lying…"

Henryk stared at the floor by the ropes where his sister fell. He stared at the spot for a long time without moving a muscle. Forty minutes later, he stood up, wiped the tears from his face, and walked out.

Adok was stunned. He didn't know what to think. It felt as if someone had stuck a knife in his heart. He didn't want to believe it. Though, he knew, it must be true.

Why would Alenka continue to challenge Ewa? There had to be a reason. Maybe Fraulein Hess put her up to it. Fraulein Hess was so bloodthirsty. Of all the frauleins, Hess was the meanest and seemed to enjoy inflicting pain the most. Adok continued to sit there, thinking and trying to figure things out. Finally, the bell sounded, and all the kids seated on the mats sprang to their feet and ran out except Adok.

"You better hurry up and wash and change for dinner. If you're late, you won't get to eat, no matter how many points you have."

Adok looked up. It was Fraulein Serena. She was walking towards him between the two mats. She didn't stop, nor did she smile at him. She merely flashed him a look going by.

Adok obeyed. A few minutes later, Adok was standing in the cafeteria. He was the tenth person in line. There were at least eight kids behind him. He looked about. He didn't see Alenka at the serving table. Glancing over his shoulder, Adok saw Henryk walk in with Casmir.

Casmir was holding onto Henryk's hand. Casmir's eyes were still red from crying, and his hair was uncombed. But he looked all right. Adok smiled and waved to him. He was eager to know how Casmir was but didn't move from his spot. Adok quickly learned that showing too much emotion and concern for others wasn't the German Way.

The line moved. Adok took a plate and filled it.

"Where's Alenka? Is she all right? Can I see her?" Fraulein, Helga nodded.

"After you get your food, you can go back and see her. She really needs a friend right now."

"The test of true friendship is to stay friends no matter what," Mr. Polanski once told him when some boys in his second-grade class refused to play with him because of his family's friendship with the Steinberg's. Adok didn't want to lose Alenka as his friend. Regardless of what happened between her and Henryk's sister, he needed to patch things up. He knew there was no way he would survive this place without her. He filled his plate and rushed into the kitchen and out the back door. He expected to find Alenka sitting at the round table under the tree. She wasn't there. The shed!

Adok ran to the wrought-iron gate and pulled. It was locked. He then carefully positioned his plate on the ledge of the brick wall and climbed over the gate. No matter what Henryk said, he knew Alenka had a good heart, and he was determined to find it.

CHAPTER TEN

Then I looked again at all the acts of oppression
which were being done under the sun.
And behold I saw the tears of the oppressed
and that they had no one to comfort them;
and on the side of their oppressors was
power, but they had no one to comfort them.

Ecclesiastes 4:1 New American Standard
Bible

Adok slowly pushed open the door to the shed.
"Alenka, where are you? Are you in here?"
The shed was dark. Even with the sunlight streaming through the open door, Adok saw only what was directly in front of him and nothing else. Adok searched the wall for the light switch. He finally found it and flipped it on. Alenka was sitting on top of a large crate in the corner. She was still wearing her gym clothes--black shorts and a white T-shirt. Usually, her blonde shoulder-length hair was neatly combed and curled under. Today it was swept to one side in a loosely braided ponytail. She looked sad and weary. Crying had left her cheeks puffy, and her eyes red and swollen. Adok could even see the tracks where her tears had rolled down her face.

"What do you want? Get out of here and leave me alone!" Alenka's voice was hard and mean. She sounded like Fraulein Hess.

"Alenka is also my mother's name. So you see, I can't leave you alone. It would be like losing my mother all over again."

"I'm not your mother."

"No, and you're not Fraulein Hess, either." "What do you know about it? You know nothing about me!"

"Then tell me, Alenka. Tell me what happened. How did you come to be here? I was climbing a tree in the park when Fraulein Hess and Franziska kidnapped me."

"Oh! How nice for you. At least you know your parents are still alive. At least you didn't…"

Alenka dropped her head, cupped her hands over her face, and cried again. Adok rushed to her side and sat down next to her on the crate. Wrapping his arms around her shoulders, he kissed her cheek and pressed his head against her forehead.

"You can tell me, Alenka. You can tell me anything. I won't tell anyone. You can trust me. Go ahead. It'll make you feel better."

Alenka lifted her head and wiped the tears from her eyes. She sighed, then shook her head. She didn't look at Adok. She spoke as if she was talking to herself.

"They killed them all, an entire village. The German soldiers lined them up and killed them. Some they chased down in the streets like they were nothing more than rats to be exterminated."

Alenka turned and looked directly at Adok.

"But they weren't rats! They were human beings, some women, but mainly boys and men, some of them as young as seventeen. My parents and grandfather, two uncles, and three male cousins were among them--the Great Kaminski's. If only my family hadn't decided to try and revive our circus act, they would be alive today. You see, a couple of years after Germany invaded Poland, the circus that my family had performed in for two generations was forced to disband because the owner was a Jew. For a year, there was no work and no money coming in.

My family didn't know how to do anything else. We were acrobats, circus people, born and raised. Even my mother had come from a circus family. She was the daughter of the Krol Kavalier's, a famous husband and wife, trick pony riding team. Having gone through what little savings we had; we were broke. So father and my uncles put on a mini circus featuring just our high-wire act and clowns. We didn't even have a tent. We had to perform outside, which made it risky because if there was a breeze, the direction and force of the wind could cause a fall. If it was raining or too windy, we canceled the show. It was all makeshift, but it was all we had, and we succeeded for a while.

My family started in April, and by June, we had performed nine shows mostly in small towns like Pile, Cozies, Wagrowiec, and Szamotuly. Katowice was our last scheduled performance. We had been playing practically nonstop since we started. My grandparents were too old to perform now. The two sold tickets and had a clown act. My grandmother, mother, and two Aunts were exhausted, and so was I, but I never complained. The only dilemma was where to stay to rest up for a week before we performed all over again. When we traveled with the circus, the crew always camped on the outskirts of town.

We never mingled with the townspeople where we held the show. The owner was adamant about that. The main reason was that it was cheaper, but the other purpose was to maintain an air of mystery. It helped that people thought of circus performers as special and unique. It drove ticket sales. But ever since the Nazi occupation, camping alongside the road or in an open field became dangerous. If caught by the SS, they automatically suspected you of being Gypsies and sent you to a concentration camp. Germans hated Gypsies almost as much as they hated Jews. So, we had to spend money to rent a place to stay. Small, rural towns were the best places to find cheap accommodations. Lidice was a friendly little village just northwest of Prague. Only, there were no public lodging places in Lidice.

After asking around, the townspeople directed us to the farmstead of the Gorski family at the far end of the village. The family was accustomed to renting out their barn to travelers. We intentionally avoided putting on a show in Prague or even stopping there because of the assassination of the SS governor, Heydrich somebody, the month before. The Gestapo was still searching for the assassins. After three days of driving nonstop from Katowice, we came upon Lidice on June 8th. We had never heard of the town before. But somehow, the Nazis concluded that the small village of Lidice had something to do with the assassination. Little did we know it would be the last place we'd ever…"

Alenka's voice cracked. She suddenly hopped down from the crate and walked around. She became distracted fiddling with the boxes and large containers as if she was interested in what may have been inside or what some might still contain. Adok watched her, bracing himself for the horror of what she would say next. It was like watching a cluster of black clouds gather in the sky and waiting for the storm to come.

Crack! Adok flinched. A small crate on top of a larger one fell on the floor, breaking the bottles inside. Alenka stared down at the broken glass and spilled liquid. Printed on one piece of a broken bottle was the word Iodine.

"This is what happened to the town of Lidice. See!"

Alenka kneeled and picked up a large piece of the crate. "This was Mr. Gorski's barn," she said, then put it down, "and these were the people, my family," she said, placing aside eleven pieces of glass from the broken bottle. She then got on her knees and rubbed her fingers in the Iodine. "This is their blood," she stated, smearing the red Iodine on her forehead and cheeks.

"I'll never forget that morning," Alenka began.

Adok noticed the strange far-away gaze in her eyes. Alenka appeared to be in a trance. She was staring into space as though she had traveled back in time, as though she was there now, reliving it all. Alenka described every sight, sound, and action in vivid detail as if she were reading from words flowing from the arteries in her heart. Her lips moved, and nothing else. She remained stoic as she revealed what happened on that day just a year ago.

"It was a perfect summer's day. You couldn't imagine, Adok, anything awful happening on a day so beautiful. There wasn't a cloud in the sky, and the glow of the sun was like a dollop of warm butter spread evenly over the land. The sound of chirping birds, mooing cows, and clucking chickens filled the air. Floating in the breeze was the sweet scent of wildflowers and garden roses mingled with the smell of freshly-cut grass, piled high in haystacks.

It was Wednesday, June 10th, and like every morning, I woke at seven o'clock sharp, automatically, without an alarm clock or the help of my mother. My three cousins, Barnum, Gallus, Ansel, and I slept up in the hayloft on blankets spread over large heaps of straw. Barnum was twenty years old, Gallus was nineteen, and Ansel was seventeen. Like my father and uncles, they had dark brown eyes and thick, wavy chestnut brown hair. They were still asleep, snoring away. I could hear the adults moving about below. As soon as I opened my eyes, I caught sight of a small sparrow perched on one of the ceiling planks. I held out my index finger and whistled to get it to come, but instead, it flew out of a crack in the roof.

I got up and rushed to open the window hatch and watched it glide across the sky. It was flying south, toward town. It flew over the main road. I was so preoccupied with watching the sparrow that I didn't notice what was happening below on the ground. It wasn't until the sparrow had flown out of sight that my eyes finally rested on the men. It looked like over a hundred were marching towards the farm, barefoot, with their hands raised high above their heads. Following slowly behind, spread across the road and open field in at least twenty jeeps, were Nazi soldiers, standing in their vehicles, pointing their rifles at the crowd of town's people.

"Oh, my God!" I raised my hand to my mouth. But before I could alert my parents, I heard the barn door open and the gruff voice of Mr. Gorski. He was a husky, broad-shouldered man with a shiny bald head and a thick black mustache.

"Go quickly! You all must leave. Hurry! The Nazis' are coming," he shouted and then ran out. Mr. Gorski hopped into his truck, where his pregnant wife, Lada, and two young sons were waiting. He sped away into the woods in the opposite direction behind the barn.

"Papa, I see them coming too!" I shouted from the hayloft.

"Wake your cousins," shouted Papa and my uncles, Fillip and Jerzy, in unison. My aunt, Nadia, Uncle Fillip's wife, became hysterical and screamed. Grandmother immediately slapped her hard across her cheek.

"No time for crying," said grandmother. Grandmother was a commanding figure. Though short and chubby, she was tough and resilient and very proud, especially of her husband and family. She had worked as a nurse in the First World War and had been in many emergency situations where a cool head was the only thing that saved a patient's life. Aunt Nadia covered her mouth and nodded. She immediately gathered her belongings, as did everyone else. My cousins had awakened and were changing out of their pajamas as was I.

After a few minutes, Papa shouted: "No! Stop! We don't have time. Leave everything, clothes, everything. We have to get out of here, right now!" Papa ordered.

Fortunately, by then, my cousins and I had changed. My cousins were all dressed in blue jeans and white T-shirts. I changed into a pink pleated cotton skirt and a white, short-sleeved blouse that buttoned down the front. I rushed to put on my white ankle socks and brown loafers. I didn't comb my hair. Before I went to bed last night, I brushed it to one side, plaited it into a single braid, and clamped the end with a white barrette. It would have to keep, for now, I thought.

My three cousins quickly climbed down from the loft, but I took one last glance out the window hatch before descending. The Germans and the crowd of men were still a considerable distance away. We had time to leave before they reached the farmhouse. Only Papa's car and my uncle's trucks were parked on the south side of the barn, visible from the road.

"Ok, everyone crouch down and enter the vehicles from the barn side only," Papa said, "then drive away quickly, straight ahead, into the woods. Drive and don't stop, no matter what happens," said Papa to his two brothers. Papa was to drive the car with mother and I and my grandparents. It was the first vehicle in the line closest to the barn door.

My father was the youngest of his brothers, yet he always took the lead, especially in a crisis. Maybe it was because his two older brothers stopped school at sixteen, which was all Polish law required. My father had completed the twelfth grade and even passed the Matura, which qualified him to go to college if he wished. He met Mama, got married, and joined the family trapeze act instead.

We bunched together and headed out. Mr. Gorski left the barn door open. But suddenly, it closed. We all froze. With frightened faces, we glanced at each other.

"The wind must have blown it shut," Papa said. "What wind?" asked Uncle Jerzy, Papa's oldest brother.

Finally, Papa went to the door. It opened easily, and he peeped out and looked around.

"Come on!" Papa waved to us.

The eleven of us followed him outside. When we reached the south side of the barn, we all ducked down and sneaked around the corner to our vehicles. The vehicles were parked one behind the other. We did as Papa said. We entered from the barn side. We continued with our heads down once inside.

Papa started his car first, then Uncle Fillip in the last truck. But Uncle Jerzy's vehicle wouldn't turn over. The engine kept clicking off. I peeped out of the window in the backseat. The crowd was still a long distance away, too far to determine if the soldiers saw us or not.

Finally, after the fifth try, Uncle Jerzy's pickup truck started, and we all drove straight ahead, heading west. As soon as our car entered the woods, my mother, grandparents, and I sat up and cheered. I glanced back at Uncle Jerzy and waved. So did my grandparents sitting next to me. We're safe; we're safe, I kept thinking. But we hadn't been driving through the woods for over ten minutes before we heard screaming. It was a woman's voice.

Everyone in the car looked around, but all we saw were trees. The shrill screams were loud enough for the whole world to hear, I thought, let alone the Nazis' back on Mr. Gorski's farm. The narrow path curved right. Immediately, we came upon Mr. Gorski's big gray truck. Both doors were open, but the car was empty. Suddenly, Mr. Gorski emerged from behind a huge pine tree.

"Help me! Help me, please! My wife is in labor. I don't know what to do." Lada Gorski was lying on a blanket on the opposite side of the tree in a long white, short-sleeved frock. Her black hair was twisted in a maiden braid and wrapped around the crown of her head. The Gorski boys, ages five and seven, were sitting on their knees beside her.

"Let me see," said grandmother. She examined Mrs. Gorski, feeling her stomach while Lada continued to cry and scream in pain.

"It's breech. The baby is coming out feet first. I must turn the baby, or both of them will die."

At first, no one said a word. But I thought we weren't far enough away to stop here. One of the

German soldiers saw our vehicles leave and would follow us. I kept looking behind us, as did my cousins.

"We don't all have to stay," said Papa.

"The rest of you can go."

"I won't leave your mother," said Grandfather firmly.

Papa nodded and turned to Mama. "I want you and Alenka to get in the truck with Jerzy and his wife, Celine, and Barnum. I'll stay here with Mama and Papa. It will be alright. As soon as the baby is born, we'll follow."

"Why must you stay? You're not the oldest," said Mother in a low voice.

"Halina," Papa said his mother's name softly, the way he always did when there was a disagreement between them.

Mother didn't answer. She just buried her head in Papa's chest while he held her in his arms, stroking the long-braided ponytail hanging down her back. The right sleeve of her blue, rose-printed dress hung off her shoulder. People always mistook my mother for my older sister. She looked much younger than her age and more Swedish than Polish, with her light blue eyes and porcelain white skin. My uncle's wives were blondes too, but neither of my aunt's hair was the same snowy blonde as my mother's and mine.

"Ahhhhhhhhh!" Mrs. Gorski's scream was even louder and more piercing than before.

"Halina," yelled grandmother, "hold her arms. Celine, hurry, find something for her to bite down on. Nadia, get another blanket and some towels."

I grabbed the Gorski boys and led them away, while my mother and aunts followed grandmother's instructions. Grandmother put her hands inside Mrs. Gorski. My mother was on her knees, leaning over the top of Lada Gorski's head and holding down her arms. Aunt Celine took Uncle Jerzy's wide, black leather belt from his pants, folded it twice, and placed it in Mrs. Gorski's mouth.

"Shh, shh, we're almost there," Grandmother assured Lada. "There!" Grandmother sighed after several minutes.

"The baby is turned." Grandmother slowly removed her hands from inside Mrs. Gorski, bringing the top of the baby's head out along too.

"Now push, push hard; the baby is almost out," said Grandmother. Mrs. Gorski grunted and pushed and pushed and grunted, biting down on Uncle Jerzy's belt until she pushed the baby's body out. After Grandfather cut the umbilical cord with the burnt edge of a razor blade, Grandmother slapped the infant's bottom. The baby cried. Aunt Nadia rushed over with a blanket from one of Gorski's suitcases and wrapped the baby in it.

"You have a beautiful little girl," said Aunt Nadia to Mr. Gorski as she handed him his daughter.

Mr. Gorski took his baby girl and placed her in his wife's arms.

"We would like to name our daughter Marcela, after you, Mrs. Kaminski," said Lada to my grandmother.

The baby had stopped crying and was lying contently in Mrs. Gorski's arms, staring up at Lada with beaming brown eyes. Grandmother just smiled and nodded as did we all. For a second, the world seemed normal and no different from any other occasion when a baby was born. The happiness of the moment overwhelmed us, and we forgot where we were. The woods surrounding us disappeared, and it was as if we were all back on the Gorski's farm, safe and secure in the prospect that our lives would go on in the days ahead exactly as the years before.

But my cousins hadn't forgotten. They were watching out for the Germans. Uncle Fillip's two sons, Gallus and Ansel, had climbed trees to warn us if they saw anyone coming. Barnum was down the road several yards away, hiding in the bushes. Suddenly, Ansel and Gallus climbed down at the same time Barnum appeared from the road.

"I think they're coming, I hear engines," said Barnum.

"We saw them, four jeeps filled with soldiers," confirmed Gallus and Ansel.

This time no one screamed. Mr. Gorski immediately picked up his wife while she was still holding their newborn and put her in his truck. I helped the Gorski boys into the back seat of their father's vehicle and ran to Papa's car. The slamming of doors and revving of engines was all that was heard. Mr. Gorski sped away so fast that he left skid marks. Papa was right behind him. I looked back and saw Uncle Fillip driving practically on top of us. He almost slammed into the back of our car, but he quickly swerved his truck off the road to the right and sped past us through the woods.

"Gustaw! Gustaw!" Papa looked in his rearview mirror when he heard his name. Everyone else in the car glanced back too. It was Uncle Jerzy, Aunt Celine, and Barnum running towards us on foot as fast as they could. Papa put the car in reverse and backed up.

"Jerzy's truck must have stalled again," said Papa. We had almost reached them when Aunt Celine fell. At first, I thought she had just slipped. But then, Uncle Jerzy fell. His head snapped backward simultaneously as his arms flew up in the air. I saw blood spurt out from the back of his head. Thump! His body hit the ground hard, and his eyes remained open as he lay motionless on the ground. Then, all at once, from between the trees, roared jeeps filled with German soldiers. Papa quickly shifted into forward drive and slammed on the gas. We sped away, but I kept looking back.

"Oh, no! Barnum! Papa!" Papa passed me a helpless glance in the rearview mirror but didn't reply. I felt a touch and looked down. Grandmother had placed her hand on top of mine. But she didn't speak or look at me. Despite the warmth of her touch, a chill ran through my body, along with the compulsion to witness my cousin's fate. I glanced back again and saw Barnum fall to his knees then raise his hands in surrender. The drivers in the jeeps kept coming at full speed. I thought they would run Barnum over. But as the last vehicle drove by, a young Nazi leaned over the side, placed his pistol to my cousin's head, and fired. I screamed. It happened so fast. The jeep never stopped or slowed down. Just like that, they killed my cousin, like he was nothing more than a shooting gallery popup target in a circus booth.

Two jeeps pursued us. The other two drove off toward Uncle Fillip's truck. The path in the woods curved left and right several times before it straightened out. The same young soldier that shot Barnum aimed his pistol at our tires, firing twice. The back tires deflated immediately, causing the car to swerve off the dirt road. Papa couldn't control it. The car zigzagged, rattled, and wobbled.

"Papa!" I screamed.

We were heading straight for a tree. Papa slammed on the brakes and stopped the car inches before impact. Papa's chin hit the steering wheel. Mama flew into the dashboard, and my grandparents and I were hurled forward into the back of the front seat. I don't remember getting out of the car. I only remember standing in line flanked by my parents and grandparents and sandwiched between my mother and grandmother.

I felt a throbbing pain in my neck and shoulders. Papa had a gash on his chin. Grandfather had a bloody nose. Mother's lower lip was also bleeding. A purplish-red bruise marked my grandmother's cheek. Eight Nazis' surrounded us. Standing directly in front of me was the young soldier who killed Barnum. He took off his helmet and looked at us. He seemed very confident and sure of himself. He stared at Mama for a long time and then at me even longer.

I didn't like the way he kept grinning and looking me up and down. He had a funny-shaped oblong face, a pointed, upturned nose, and thin lips. His eyes were light blue. His hair was as yellow as the sun. He was even younger than I first thought.

Up close, he looked to be just a boy of sixteen, which was the youngest any male could join the army. He was only an inch taller than me. At twelve, I stood five feet. But he was cocky. No one could tell him he wasn't ten feet tall. He strutted up to me and stroked the tip of my braid. I winced and pulled away from him. I kept seeing his thin, grubby fingers pulling the trigger and shooting Barnum. The thought of those same fingers touching me now made me sick to my stomach. Repulsed, I slapped his hand away and spat in his face. The young soldier quickly reacted and reached for his pistol.

"No!" screamed my mother and grandparents. Mama quickly grabbed me and shielded me partially behind her back. Papa also tried to come to my assistance but was stopped by a gun placed directly against the back of his head by one of the soldiers standing behind us. I was scared and thought the boy soldier would kill me too. Instead, he chuckled and released his hand from the trigger.

My saliva landed on his top lip. He didn't wipe my spit off with his hand. He licked it off with his tongue, then puckered his mouth and blew me a kiss. Drawing back his head, he let out a full-throated laugh, and this time, the other soldiers all joined in. They were still laughing when Uncle Fillip, Aunt Nadia, Gallus, and Ansel appeared on foot with their hands behind their heads.

Two jeeps followed behind them with soldiers pointing their guns. My uncle and his family joined us in line.

"Bewegen Sie schnell auf diese Weise!" said a much older soldier standing in one jeep that had just arrived.

He was pointing toward Gorski's farm. The soldier holding a gun to Papa's head pushed him forward. We all walked behind each other in a single file. As we got closer to the farm, we heard gunfire. The gunfire came at regular intervals. Sometimes it was single shots of five in rapid succession. Sometimes it was a flurry of machine gunfire. The shooting started, then stopped, and after a few minutes, commenced again.

We finally reached the spot where our vehicles had entered the woods. The familiar sight of Mr. Gorski's white stucco, gambrel-roof barn, was directly ahead of us. German military cars were parked all around it. Mattresses filled two trucks parked on each side of the closed barn doors where soldiers stood guard. Some cushions taken off the villager's beds still had bed sheets on them.

The men from the town were standing in a long line directly in front of the barn door as if they were waiting to enter a theatre to see a picture show. They were being marched inside in groups of five. Each group of men retrieved a mattress from one truck before entering. Under guard, a group of townsmen was digging a huge ditch several yards away on the south side of the barn. As soon as we reached the barn, the soldiers tried to separate us. The soldiers ushered Papa, grandfather, Uncle Fillip, and my two cousins to the back of the line with the other men. They pulled my mother, grandmother, Aunt Nadia and I away and ordered us into the back of an empty pickup truck. Only, grandmother wouldn't go. She wouldn't leave grandfather and hit the cocky, young soldier who shot Barnum in his chest with her fists.

"No! Leave me alone. I stay with my husband," Grandmother yelled. For a sixty-five-year-old woman, Grandmother was strong. She was too big for the boy soldier to handle. She had big bones and heavy hands. During the struggle, Grandmother drew back her arm and swung. She swiped the boy soldier across the face so hard his helmet flew off his head, and he stumbled backward. When he bent down to retrieve his helmet, grandmother bumped her big, round butt into his small butt and sent the cocky soldier plummeting face down in the dirt. It was the exact stunt my grandparents performed in one of their clown acts. It always got lots of laughs. It did this time, too. Everyone erupted into laughter, even the soldiers.

"Shut up!" yelled the boy soldier. His face was cherry red. He got up off the ground and drew his pistol. When he shoved it into grandmother's cheek, all the laughter stopped. Mother, Aunt Nadia, and I were standing in front of the truck's back end. I grabbed hold of my mother's hand and held my breath. Words spit out of the soldier's mouth fast and furious as he held his finger on the trigger. "Sie polnische Kuh des Fettes! Ich möchte sehen, dass wie viel jeder lacht, nachdem brenne ich durch, gehen Sie hässlich weg! "voran."

As much as I could understand, he called grandmother a fat Polish cow and would blow her ugly head off.

"Halt! Lassen Sie sie sein. Wenn die fette polnische Kuh es vorzieht, entlang Seite geschossen zu werden ihr Ehemann, lassen Sie."

Everyone turned to see who was ordering the young soldier to stand down. When the German soldiers saw the officer, they all snapped to attention and stood as straight and stiff as stone pillars.

We each let out a gasp upon seeing that the officer was a woman. That was the first time I laid eyes on Fraulein Hess. She was so beautiful, not because she was the most attractive woman I ever saw—my mother was much prettier. But there was an aura about her, a regal air. She exuded pride and self-confidence. I could tell just by looking at her that she wasn't afraid of anything. Even my grandmother looked impressed.

The fraulein's golden blonde hair cascaded over her shoulders under a white officer's side cap with silver piping. There was a round tri-colored cockade embroidered on the band. She wore tan leather, lace-up boots, and white gabardine Jodhpur trousers with a matching white, long-sleeved jacket that buttoned down the front. Two boxed-pleated breast pockets were adorned with silver-pebble buttons on both sides of the coat. A large silver and black metal cross was pinned to the left breast pocket. Above the right breast pocket was a silver eagle, clutching a swastika. Strapped to her waist was a black leather gun holster.

The female officer walked up to my grandmother. "My name is Captain Dagmar Hess of the Women's

Auxiliary Air Force, the Luftwaffe Artillery Division." Her voice was sharp but calm and dignified. "I applaud your willingness to stand with your husband. It takes strength and courage to do so and should be admired. Come, let me escort you."

Fraulein Hess held out her arm. Grandmother linked arms with the captain as she led Grandmother to the back of the line beside Grandfather. The fraulein was six feet tall and walked with her chin up as straight and as commanding as any male officer. All the townsmen in line bowed their heads when Fraulein Hess approached as if she were royalty.

Grandfather took grandmother by the hand, kissed her forehead, and bowed his head to the captain, as did my father, uncle, and two cousins. No one said a word. Fraulein Hess merely nodded back in recognition of their respect. She then turned and was about to walk away in the other direction when she noticed my mother and me. She walked over to us. She smelled of Ginger Blossoms. The fragrance was subtle and refreshing, like a summer's breeze.

Smiling down at us, she looked Mother and me over carefully. She touched the loose curl hanging over Mother's eye, then stroked the tip of my braid. "The two of you have excellent features, and both of you are so young and pretty--sisters?"

"No. This is my daughter," Mother replied with an edge in her voice mingled with a tinge of arrogance. I looked at Mama, wondering why her tone was so curt as did Aunt Nadia, standing beside me. Fraulein Hess noticed it, too, and moved closer. Her mood quickly changed. Her jaw stiffened. Her eyes narrowed. Her cheeks became taut and drawn. Her lips curled into a snarl. When she leaned over and stared into Mama's eyes, a quiver ran through me. Fraulein Hess was leaning so far into Mama's face that Mother had to bend back to prevent the two from butting heads.

"Since you can produce such beautiful children, we must make sure you produce more of them." Fraulein Hess snapped her fingers. The nearest soldier came running to her side. The captain straightened her posture.

"The men can have this one for lunch. Pass the word around," she told the soldier without taking her eyes off Mama. She reached over, grabbed my braid, and yanked me to her side. I fought her, kicking and crying. As I was pulled away, I heard my mother scream, and my father shouted: "No, fraulein, no! Please stop!"

Everyone in my family was yelling now at the top of their lungs. Somehow, Aunt Nadia reached the fraulein and me without being apprehended by one of the soldiers who had seized my mother and the rest of my family.

"Please, captain, Madame, sir. Please, my sister-in-law didn't mean it. Jealousy, that's why she responded the way she did. She's always been a little jealous. You know how some women can be when they see another woman reach a position above what is considered to be a woman's place. Please forgive her. Please, don't let this happen! My sister-in-law has German ancestry, you know, on her mother's side." Aunt Nadia was begging Captain Hess, holding onto the captain's arm.

I wrapped my arms around the captain's waist, displaying all the affection I could muster toward her. For a moment, it seemed our effort to soften the captain was working. She stopped walking and dragging me away when Aunt Nadia revealed Mama's heritage. My mother's grandmother was German, born in Frankfurt.

Fraulein Hess looked down at me. Standing on my tiptoes, I reached up to kiss her cheek. She responded by bending down to meet my kiss. But the moment my lips touched her face, a flurry of gunshots rang out—bang, burr bang, burr bang, rattle-tat-tat.

Aunt Nadia screamed the names of her husband and sons. I froze in place, afraid to look back. I didn't have to. I no longer heard my parents' voices and knew I would never hear them again. I only heard Aunt Nadia's voice now.

"You evil, Nazi witch!" Aunt Nadia lunged at the captain, hissing like a cat. Captain Hess quickly pulled her pistol from her holster and shot Aunt Nadia twice in the stomach at close range. I stepped back and watched. The force of the gunfire propelled my aunt backward. She landed two feet away.

Aunt Nadia lay still with her eyes closed and her blonde hair spread over the dirt like a blanket. Two large bloodstains saturated her yellow cotton dress. Tears filled the corners of her eyes.

Fraulein Hess turned and looked down at me. The look on her face was seething. The weight of her stare sent a shiver through my veins, and suddenly, my legs gave out. I felt myself falling, and then I felt myself being lifted. The scent of Ginger Blossoms filled my nostrils, mingled with the smell of blood and gun smoke. As Fraulein Hess carried me away, I lay stiff, listless, and too weak to move. With my head tilted back against the captain's arm, all I saw was blue. I spotted a sparrow flying across the sky, and my mind flashed back. I couldn't help but wonder if it was the same sparrow I saw in Mr. Gorski's barn this morning.

If only I could fly, I thought. If only people could fly away whenever they were in danger, the sky would be filled with humans now, all fleeing for their lives.

Fraulein Hess put me in the back seat of a car, tapped a soldier on his shoulder, and we drove away. I was still lying in the captain's arms, but too afraid to look at her. I stared at the car roof instead. Fraulein Hess stroked my braid.

"I will be your mother now," she whispered. Her empathic voice was soothing. She even sounded like my mother. I lowered my gaze until my eyes fell upon her face. I couldn't help it. I cried. Fraulein Hess lifted my head to her bosom.

I responded and wrapped my arms around her neck. Being held felt good. For the first time that day, I felt safe. I closed my eyes, imagining I was in my mother's arms. I could have kept them shut forever, but the car hit a bump, and my eyes popped open involuntarily. Suddenly, I was looking out the back window. I saw the barn in the distance and the vague images of soldiers dropping bodies into a ditch. A spot of yellow and then of blue flashed before my eyes, then disappeared."

Adok didn't know how long he had been crying or when, during Alenka's story, he started. Tears drenched his face and shirt. In his mind's eye, he saw everything Alenka relayed as clearly as if he had been with her. For a while, there was silence. Then Alenka rose abruptly off the floor and walked around the shed, smashing and knocking over all the crates and boxes she could.

"You're right, Adok. Fraulein Hess isn't my mother," said Alenka, between tipping over containers. "She's just what Aunt Nadia called her, an evil, Nazi witch! And I hate her; I hate them all. Who gave Germans the right to go around killing people and to determine who was worthy of living and dying? The Bible says God created man. Nowhere in the Bible does it say that God created Germans first, and every other race must subject themselves to their dictates and approval?"

A shadow appeared outside the door while Alenka was speaking. Someone was listening at the entrance. Adok noticed the figure when Alenka proclaimed her hatred of Fraulein Hess. He saw the shadow from the corner of his eye, but he dared not look. He knew who it was without looking. The moment he spoke the name in his head, Alenka stopped what she was doing and turned towards the door as if she had heard him say the name Fraulein Hess out loud.

Fraulein Hess stepped into view and then inside. Alenka backed away. Adok slid off the crate but didn't move. Suddenly, the shed got stuffy and too hot to breathe as if it had caught on fire and was filling up with smoke.

"Adok, leave," ordered Fraulein Hess in a low growl with her right hand clutching her gun belt. In defiance, Adok balled his fists. He was determined not to be afraid and abandoned Alenka to face Fraulein Hess alone.

"Whatever you do to her, you'll have to do to me, too," he said.

"A-DOK!"

His name roared out of her throat like a crack of thunder. The sheer force of it made Adok flinch, and he fell, stumbling over his feet.

"Go on, Adok, I'm not afraid anymore," said Alenka. Her voice was calm and resolute as her eyes remained fixed on Fraulein Hess.

Adok stood up and kissed Alenka on her cheek before walking cautiously towards the door.

"Don't hurt her!" He shouted to Fraulein Hess. His voice squeaked with emotion. Turning sideways, he made his way towards the door. He was sure Fraulein Hess would swat him, but she didn't even look at him as he slid by her. As soon as he stepped outside, Fraulein Hess slammed the door shut behind him. Adok waited at the door for a while, trying to hear what was happening inside. He couldn't, so he slowly walked towards the wrought iron gate, crying. He was imagining the punishment Fraulein Hess was administering to Alenka shut up in the shed.

"Oh, God! Please, help her, help her!" He prayed. Fraulein Helga and Serena immediately popped into his head. Adok shot through the gate. He knew that they were the only two who could save Alenka now.

CHAPTER ELEVEN

"One lives in the hope of becoming a memory."

Antonio Porchia

Every afternoon at three o'clock, all the frauleins gathered in the parlor on the main floor for tea. It was a pink room furnished with white wicker sofas and chairs upholstered in red damask. Children were forbidden to enter unless invited by one fraulein as a reward for high achievement or good behavior. Since arriving at the Lebensborn Home at Kinder Ausleselager camp last year, Alenka has always been present for tea with the Frauleins. Today, she was not.

Nearly out of breath, Adok rushed into the parlor. "Fraulein Helga, you must come now. Alenka's in trouble. She's with your sister, locked in the shed.

I'm afraid your sister will kill her!"

Fraulein Helga was sitting on the sofa in front of the window, holding a cup of tea. Sitting beside her was Fraulein Franziska.

"Don't exaggerate, little boy. A parent has the right to discipline their children, and a mother wouldn't kill her child," said Franziska.

"Alenka's not her child, and you know it," replied Adok.

Fraulein Franziska's eyes narrowed. She was about to respond when Fraulein Helga finally spoke. "But my sister loves Alenka like a daughter. She has from the beginning. I remember the day she arrived with her. My sister was so attentive to Alenka. I've never seen her behave that way toward any other child. My sister boasted about how pretty Alenka was and how she was the perfect little Aryan girl. She still boasts and…"

"Captain Hess is Alenka's mother," Fraulein Franziska interrupted.

"She filed adoption papers three months ago and just received confirmation of the adoption today. The captain got permission from the Fuhrer to adopt Alenka without being married. She went to find Alenka to tell her the great news. Also, when the war is over, no matter which side wins, Captain Hess plans to take Alenka to South America with her to live, and I'm going with them."

Adok was speechless. He didn't know what to think. If this were true, then Fraulein Hess wouldn't hurt Alenka. But the angry look on the captain's face said something different.

Adok stood there, wondering what to do. Then Fraulein Serena burst into the room, screaming frantically.

"I heard shots in the shed! I went out to read under the tree, and I heard two shots just as I sat down. I ran to open the door, but it was locked from the inside. I couldn't find the key on the kitchen latch."

"I have a spare key," said Helga. Everyone ran out. Adok led the way. When they reached the shed, he snatched the key from Fraulein Helga's hand and unlocked the door.

Inside was a bloody scene. Fraulein Hess and Alenka lay cater-corner to one another. Two streams of blood from their bodies merged into one big puddle at the door's entrance. Adok and Serena ran to Alenka, Helga, and Franziska to Fraulein Hess. The other Frauleins stood in the doorway looking on.

Alenka was on her back, her head tilted toward the ceiling, and her arms spread out to her sides. Blood from the gunshot wound to her upper chest stained her white T-shirt. Adok trembled as he stared down at her body. He couldn't take his eyes off her Iodine-smeared face. She looked peaceful, as if she was just in a deep, restful sleep and not dead. He felt sick to his stomach, but no tears were in his eyes. Instead, he imagined himself climbing a tree with Alenka on his back and her arms and legs wrapped around his neck and waist. She felt so light, as if she weighed nothing. She was giggling in his ear and urging him to climb even higher. He did until they reached the top. There, the two became one with the night sky.

For hours, it seemed, they floated among the stars with the shimmering glow of the full moon as their pillow. But Alenka slipped, a little bit at first, and then all at once, she fell and was holding onto Adok's legs. Adok reached down to lift her up, but she was gone.

Alenka! Alenka!

"Alenka! Alenka!" Fraulein Hess's voice was weak and raspy. She was shot in the stomach and strained to lift her head. Helga placed her arm under her sister's head, lifting it slightly off the floor.

"She told me I could never be her mother and that she hated me. I handed her my pistol and told her if she hated me so much, then shoot. She pointed the gun at me, but I knew she couldn't. Then she turned the pistol on herself. I grabbed it. We struggled. It went off. As I was falling, I heard another shot."

With tears in her eyes, Fraulein Hess peered over at Alenka's body. She coughed and spit blood.

"My beautiful Aryan daughter," Fraulein Hess whispered before her eyes lowered and her head dropped forward.

CHAPTER TWELVE

"Nothing is so painful to the human
mind as a great and sudden change."

Mary Shelley

Things were never the same after the deaths
of Alenka and Fraulein Hess. Not even Fraulein
Franziska had the desire to continue as before. She
relinquished her duties as next in line to run the
Lebensborn Home to Fraulein Serena. Grief-stricken
over losing her best friend, Fraulein Franziska walked
about weeping and mumbling to herself for several
months until a doctor found her mentally unstable and
admitted her to a hospital.

Many of the other frauleins left. Out of twenty-
seven, twelve remained. Fraulein Helga stayed on as
the cook.

"Where else am I to go," she said. "Now that my
sister's gone, I have no one."

For the children, things got better. Fraulein Serena
eliminated the strict rules that enforced German
allegiance and fostered Jewish hatred.

Everyone ate three meals a day, every day, no
matter what. Fraulein Serena ran the home like an
actual orphanage.

Every Saturday, parents wanting to adopt visited to view the children. Casmir was the first adopted. Others followed. Every three or four weeks, at least one couple selected a child, and sometimes more than one child was chosen. It took three months for the adoption to go through. Whenever Fraulein Serena located a child's birth parents, they went home.

Henryk was one of those lucky ones. The following year, he was put on a train and returned to his home in Poznan, Poland. Serena had no luck finding information on Adok's parents. With Casmir and Henryk gone, Adok spent most of his playtime alone. Months after Alenka died, Adok dreamed of the two climbing a tree every night. Sometimes, when they reached the top, a face on the moon appeared and winked and smiled down at them. Sometimes, a star fell, and they caught it and held it in their hands. But shortly afterward, Alenka slipped and then disappeared, and Adok woke up sad, missing her even more.

During the day, Fraulein Serena kept him busy with schoolwork and weekly chores—no more Nazi indoctrination. In school, they studied science, math, history, and literature.

Of the four, Adok liked literature the most because he often found in the writings of others exactly how he felt but couldn't express. The study of world literature introduced Adok to American writers. Edgar Allen Poe became his favorite. As his first assignment, Adok recited the poem, The Raven, from memory, which was quite a feat since it was eighteen stanzas long. Fraulein Serena's favorite poem was Splendor in the

Grass by an English poet named William Wordsworth. She made Adok memorize it, too.

"The Raven " is a magnificent poem but much too dark and gloomy. It does nothing to uplift and revive the spirit. So, I want you to memorize my poem. It's much shorter, and as you grow up, I think it will serve you better."

Adok didn't want to, but he memorized it to please her. Fraulein Serena was a good friend. He loved her. But no one could ever take Alenka's place. Two years after her death, Adok mourned her even more than the day she died. The passing of time didn't ease his pain or lessen the overwhelming sense of loss he felt. Instead of forgetting her, he was thinking about her more and more. He grew to resent Alenka for committing suicide and leaving him all alone.

That resentment sometimes made him mean and angry. Adok got mad and screamed at the other children for no reason. If one boy accidentally brushed up against him, Adok got into a fight with him. If one boy knocked over their glass of milk, he screamed at him as if the boy had spilled his.

"It's not just Alenka you're missing; it's your mother, too," said Fraulein Serena. "You associate Alenka with her. That's logical since they both have the same name. That's also why you feel a greater sense of loss. But it would be best to calm down, Adok, being angry won't help. You must learn to draw strength from tragedy, face your present situation, and look beyond it. This war will not last forever. From the way it's going now, a German defeat is inevitable.

When that happens, you'll be able to leave here and reunite with your parents."

Adok wanted to go now. He thought about running away every day. But he didn't want to leave that way. It would cause Fraulein Serena and Helga too much worry and hurt. It would also show a lack of appreciation for all they had done for him.

What he appreciated most was that neither of them tried to take his mother's or Alenka's place. The relationship between the three was more like that between an older sister and a brother and an aunt and a nephew.

Still, every day, he became increasingly restless and eager to leave. On Friday, April 20, 1945, Adok finally got his wish. The day started like any other: up at five o'clock, breakfast at 5:30, drills from six to seven, and school from 7:15 until 11:45. Lunch was at noon. After lunch, there were physical training classes.

The first activity Adok performed in the gym was rope climbing. He regularly timed himself to see how fast he could go up and down. That day was no different. He was climbing when a hush suddenly fell over the gymnasium. Once he reached the top, Adok looked down and saw all the children standing straight and still, the way they used to when Fraulein Hess was in charge, and she and the other Frauleins entered the room.

Adok almost fell when he saw why. Four very stern-looking SS soldiers stood at the door as if guarding it. Adok could hear his heart beating faster. He hadn't felt this afraid in a long time.

The familiar feeling of foreboding swept over him all at once.

Fraulein Serena and Helga stood between the soldiers. Next to them was a short, fragile-looking old man wearing round, gold-rim glasses. Beside him was a bony young man with red hair dressed in what looked like blue and white striped pajamas. The young man didn't appear to be in his right mind and was swaying back and forth. When Adok saw the old man pointing at him, he stopped breathing. The four walked towards him, leaving the soldiers at the door. Although the young man was dragging his left foot, he kept up.

"Adok, come down, please," requested Fraulein Serena.

Adok loosened his grip and slid down the rope.

"This gentleman, Professor Josef Weiss, is looking for someone to be a companion to his nephew, who has suffered some brain damage as a result of being taken by mistake to a concentration camp and badly mistreated."

"How old are you, son?" asked the old man.

"Ten-years-old sir."

"Well, you are quite a little climber. You jimmied up that rope in no time. Do you like to climb?"

"Yes, sir, though I prefer climbing trees. The frauleins won't let me, though. They are afraid I'll fall."

The old man was staring at Adok with a gleam in his eyes. He reached out and touched the thick, curly blonde locks on Adok's head.

"What a good-looking boy you are," he said admiringly.

"What is your nephew's name? Adok asked. Adok noticed the innocent, dejected look in the young man's eyes. It was the look of a child who had seen and experienced the cruelty and inhumanity of adults they should have trusted and who should have protected them. It reminded him of the look he saw on Alenka's face in the shed the day she died.

"His name is Hans," said the professor. "Unfortunately, my nephew also lost his voice, as well."

"And how old is he?"

"He just turned eighteen two days ago," the professor said. Adok smiled at Hans. He liked him. Hans smiled back.

"Well, it looks like the two of you are going to get along just fine," said Professor Weiss. "This is the first time I've seen Hans smile at anything or anyone since I rescued him three weeks ago. So, would you like to come with us? This is the third Lebensborn Home we've been to today, and it would be a great relief to me if I didn't have to go to another."

Adok tried not to appear too eager, noticing the doleful looks on Fraulein Serena and Helga's faces.

"Yes, I think so."

Fraulein Serena was about to speak, but Helga shook her head from side-to-side and glanced back at the four SS soldiers. Serena glanced back at them, too, and then nodded with a sigh.

"Good! Now, can you pack as quickly as you jimmied up that rope?"

"Yes, sir!" Adok beamed and raced away to the boy's dormitory. Fraulein Serena hurried after him. When she entered, Adok was already putting into a straw suitcase a spinning top, his favorite toy, picturing circus clowns and acrobats that Serena gave him for his birthday last year. It reminded Adok of Alenka's family. He placed it on top of the few clothes issued to him since his stay here. Fraulein Serena had bought all the children a small suitcase in case they were adopted.

"Adok, I don't like this. I know you want to leave, but there's something suspicious about this professor and this entire situation. Who really is he, and why does a common, ordinary teacher need to be escorted by four SS soldiers to select a boy to be a playmate for his nephew? Don't you think that's odd?"

Adok didn't answer. He just closed the suitcase, fastened the latches then grabbed the handle. "I'm ready," he said, glancing over at Fraulein Serena sitting on the edge of his bed. Fraulein Serena drew him into her arms and hugged him. Adok wrapped his arms around her neck and hugged her back.

"I don't want to let you go, but I know I must." She then cupped his face between her hands and kissed his forehead and both cheeks gently before releasing him.

"All right," she said as she stood up. "Come on."

Taking hold of Adok's free hand, Serena walked him outside to the front entrance, where the professor and his nephew were waiting. As soon as Adok saw Fraulein Helga ran up to her and hugged her too.

"Goodbye, Auntie," he said. Fraulein Helga wiped the tears from her eyes, then shook his hand and kissed Adok on both cheeks.

"You were just a little boy when you came here two years ago. And although you're still just a child, you've grown so much older. Good luck, and may God bless and keep you safe, Adok Makowski."

"Don't worry, frauleins, either of you," said Professor Weiss, "If I have anything to do with it, Adok will have a healthy, prosperous life and live a long, long time. I guarantee it, whether God has anything to do with it or not."

Adok climbed into the backseat with the professor and Hans and closed the door. Two SS soldiers sat waiting in the front seat. The other two soldiers were on motorcycles. The soldier on the passenger's side nodded to the soldier driving, who then bowed to the soldiers on motorbikes. Together, they all started their engines simultaneously and slowly pulled away. Adok fought his back tears.

Don't look back. You wanted to leave. Don't look back. Adok told himself that he must be a big boy about it now.

But unable to help himself, Adok stuck his head out the window, put his right hand to his lips, and blew kisses to Fraulein Serena and Helga. The two were still standing in front of the building, their arms linked and their free hand waving goodbye to him.

"I love you!" he shouted, waving back vigorously. He waved until their images disappeared in the distance and then pulled his head back inside. He didn't wipe his face. He didn't mind the tears. It felt good to cry.

He wanted to lock this moment in his memory forever. Suddenly feeling tired, He leaned back and closed his eyes. Immediately, the words of Fraulein Serena's favorite poem by William Wordsworth came to mind:

What though the radiance which was once so bright. Be now forever taken from my sight. Though nothing can bring back the hour of splendor in the grass, of glory in the flower, we will grieve not, rather find strength in what remains behind.

Adok opened his eyes. He was startled by the warmth of another person's skin against his. He looked down and saw the hand of the professor's nephew clutching his fingers.

CHAPTER THIRTEEN

"Sometimes you wake up. Sometimes the fall kills you. And sometimes when you fall, you fly.

Neil Gaiman

1:00 AM, May 1, 1945.
Burg Rottlen Castle, Germany

"How did he climb up there without a ladder?" Colonel Strauss asked, gazing up at Adok, clinging to the wall with only his fingertips and bare feet. The boy was high enough to touch the twenty-foot-tall ceiling.

"We don't know. Adok was eating his third helping of kielbasa and sauerkraut. Private Dag and I were smoking and talking over there by the window when the doctor's nephew started clapping.

We turned around and saw the boy scaling the wall," explained Arnulf.

Dr. Weiss smiled as he peered up at Adok. "Amazing," he whispered to himself.

Adok looked down at them and laughed. "Come down, come down right now, I order you!"

Colonel Strauss shouted, then turned to Dr. Weiss. "Is this the result of the serum? If so, it has made him crazy. Look at him; he's mad!"

"He is not crazy, Kommandant, I assure you; over-exuberant, yes, but far from crazy."

Still laughing, Adok shouted: "Look at me, look at me; see, you can't get me now, ha, ha, ha."

"That's enough, Adok. You've had your fun, now come down, son," yelled Dr. Weiss.

"No! And you can't make me," Adok screamed back.

"I can make you," said Colonel Strauss. He drew his pistol, aimed it up at Adok, and fired.

"Ha, ha--you missed." Adok stuck out his tongue.

The Colonel fired again.

"Kommandant, please, stop! That won't help," said Dr. Weiss.

"Don't worry; I'm not trying to hit him. I'm just trying to scare the boy down."

The colonel then raised his gun again. Just as he was about to shoot, Hans slapped his hand, knocking it upward. The gun went off anyway. The bullet ricocheted off the ceiling beam and hit Adok dead center in the back.

"Ouch, what was that?!" Adok yelled before tumbling to the floor like a falling tree branch.

Thump! Adok landed on his back.

Everyone gathered around him. Adok's arms were spread out like an eagle, and one of his legs was bent under the other.

Hans fell to his knees and wept and shook Adok's body.

"Shh, shh, Hans, it's all right. He's not dead," assured his uncle.

"He's not breathing," said Dag.

Arnulf agreed. "From a fall that high, he's got to be dead."

"When did the two of you become doctors?" Colonel Strauss questioned. "Get out, both of you!"

The two privates hesitated.

"That's an order!" The colonel commanded.

"Yes sir," they saluted, clicked their heels, and left.

"Let's get him back on the operating table," said Dr. Weiss.

Carefully, Hans picked up Adok and placed him on the bed. Colonel Strauss noticed the bullet on the floor where Adok's body had been lying and picked it up. A speck of blood covered it. Strauss handed it to the doctor.

Dr. Weiss held the bullet in his palm and examined it before putting it into the pocket of his white coat. He then examined Adok. He felt a split in Adok's skull, starting from the center and running down the back of his head.

"He's cracked his skull, but there's no blood."

"How long will it take him to come back to life?"

Dr. Weiss looked at his watch.

"It's one-thirty now. I would say the boy has been dead at least two minutes already, so…"

"Hmm, hmm," Adok's arms and legs twitched.

"Mama, Alenka," he moaned, moving his head slowly from side-to-side before his eyes opened. Adok sat up.

"How does your head feel?"

Adok rubbed his forehead. "A little heavy, like something hard, is pressing against it, but it doesn't hurt."

"Can you feel a wound?" asked Dr. Weiss.

"No," Adok said after running his hand from the top to the back of his skull. Dr. Weiss rechecked Adok's skull. The split was no longer there.

"Good. You'll be fine," said Dr. Weiss, grinning.

The doctor looked at the colonel, also smiling.

Hans became agitated and plodded his way toward the small window.

"He hears something," said the doctor. "Gunfire," said Colonel Strauss after listening more carefully. The colonel hurried past Hans to the small window. He unhooked the window latch, opened the window, and looked down, beaming his flashlight. Dr. Weiss followed the colonel over to the window to look for himself. All the soldiers in the courtyard were shooting at something or someone.

Suddenly Arnulf and Dag rushed into the room. "Colonel Strauss, sir, the-the…" Arnulf was huffing and puffing, trying to catch his breath.

"The Negro soldier that fell out the window is in the courtyard killing soldiers with his bare hands," Arnulf blurted out finally.

"But no one can kill him," Dag piped in. "No matter how many times they shoot him, he doesn't die."

"Mein Got! He's going to kill us all. Quickly, we must leave. I know a secret passage. Follow me," said Dr. Weiss.

CHAPTER FOURTEEN

Cowards die many times before their deaths;
the valiant never taste of death but once.

William Shakespeare

The moon loomed above the Thirteenth Century Castle. The ominous sight appeared surreal to Sergeant Johnson. It was like a clip from a horror movie. It even had a drawbridge. Kapp kept his head down as he quietly crossed the bridge and crouched behind bushes. A campfire blazed in the center of the open courtyard. At least thirty or more Nazis' camped out across the grounds. A convoy of soldiers in jeeps and on foot passed him. Kapp realized they were searching for him. He didn't blink until every soldier crossed the bridge and disappeared into the forest.

Kapp's head told him there were too many Jerries to take alone. He needed to sneak into the castle without being seen. But he couldn't wait. Every bone in his body was a lightning bolt transmitting power and energy to his soul. Overwhelmed by the sensation, Kapp felt driven and wanted to attack now. He would kill them all. He knew it. Without making a sound, he slowly rose from behind the bushes. Twenty-feet away, three Jerries stood laughing and smoking cigarettes. Kapp rushed them, armed with nothing more than his tightly clenched fists. He landed the first blow to the back of a Jerries' head before the other Jerries noticed him. The soldier was dead before his body hit the ground.

German officers blew their whistles. "Schwarze soldat! Get him! Kill him!"

Every Jerry rushed toward Kapp with rifles drawn, encircling him. Kapp heard a bullet whisk past his ear. He turned to his right and spotted a shooter standing on the hood of a jeep. The shooter fired another shot. Kapp immediately felt the bullet penetrate the center of his forehead. As soon as the bullet entered, the blood in his entire body percolated in his veins before the bullet popped out and dropped on the ground next to his bare feet. The stunned Germans surrounding Kapp backed away. Some ran away. Others became frantic and shot off their rifles at Kapp in rapid succession. But hit or miss, Kapp didn't die. He fought them all like a raging bull, ramming and goring his fists into their guts with such ferocity that clumps of blood spurted out of their nose and mouth. The Jerries fell one by one until Kapp Ulysses Johnson was the only soldier standing.

The Sergeant looked around at the bodies lying on the ground. The number of dead Nazis was too many to count, and he didn't try. Instead, he rubbed his hands over his chest, arms, and legs. His shirt was full of bullet holes. He ripped it off and flung it on the ground. Amazingly, his body was free of gunshots--no wounds, no scars. The impact of the bullets puncturing his flesh caused a faint stinging and nothing more. Kapp gently rubbed the place on his forehead where the first bullet entered. He didn't understand how he was still alive. But he knew something inside him had changed. Kapp felt different. An exhilarating tingling sensation surged through his body, making him feel invincible. He liked the feeling.

Kapp entered the castle through a massive oak door and walked into an expansive room dimly lit by candlelight. Off the great hall were rooms, doorways, and arched hallways. Kapp hesitated, unsure of where to go. He started toward one door and spotted a small entryway tucked in a corner. He took it.

The tunnel-like hallway was dark and narrow. Kapp could barely see as he walked, but he soon heard footsteps coming his way. He stopped. It was the sound of running feet directly ahead of him. Kapp kept listening. The noise wasn't getting louder but weaker. Kapp hurried down the corridor. When he heard voices, he slowed down.

"Come along, Adok. We must hurry," said the voice of an old man.

"No! I don't want to! I want to go home!" cried the child.

"Pick him up and carry him if you must!"

Kapp reacted to the voice giving the order and stopped. He recognized it as the voice of the Nazi colonel in the tower. Kapp ran. He was determined to catch up to them and kill the colonel and all the soldiers with him.

"What do you hear, Hans?" asked Dr. Weiss. "Is someone coming?"

Suddenly, Kapp saw a light shining in the distance. "I can't see anyone," Kapp heard another voice say.

Don't point that flashlight in that direction, you fool!" The colonel ordered. "Keep moving."

Kapp continued until he tripped and tumbled down a long flight of stone steps. He landed on his back on the hard dirt floor. Kapp looked up and saw the moon glowing through an elongated slot at the top of the wall. It was a view he had seen before. Kapp realized this was where he and his brother Pauli had been held. He stood up.

He told himself they couldn't have gotten out by climbing up there.

Kapp felt along the walls for another exit. He stepped on something and lifted his foot. It was a silver chain. Kapp picked up the chain and held it up to the moonlight. The tiny ball-link chain was like the one he wore around his neck. Only it was missing the identification tags. Kapp scanned the dirt floor in search of what had been hanging from the chain. It wasn't easy to see the moon as the only light source. He continued anyway, desperate to find what he believed were his stepbrother's dog tags.

Finally, Kapp came to a raised area in the dirt. He immediately got down on his knees and ran his hands over the mound. He estimated the pile to be around five feet, nine inches long, about the height of his baby brother. Kapp became frantic and dug with his bare hands. He found one of his brother's dog tags and dug even faster until the head and torso of Pauli were exposed.

Staring at the corpse, Kapp could not contain his grief. The fire had disfigured the body. The pungent odor of burnt flesh was still smoldering from the carcass. Tearing up, Kapp drew back his head and screamed. The roar of his cries was so loud they echoed through the castle halls and traveled far beyond its ancient stone walls, penetrating even the dense woods of the Black Forest.

CHAPTER FIFTEEN

Deep into the darkness peering, long
I stood there wondering, fearing, doubting,
dreaming dreams no mortal ever
dared to dream before.

Edgar Allen Poe

Colonel Strauss sat in the back seat to the right of Dr. Weiss in a military jeep while being driven by Private Dag Narvik down a two-lane highway. On the opposite side of Dr. Weiss sat Adok between the doctor and his nephew, Hans. They had not been driving for over twenty minutes when the sixteen-year-old soldier stopped the jeep on the road and clicked off the engine. Everyone sat motionless, listening. An eerie, screeching sound was settling upon the night air like a thick fog.

"You hear that?" asked Dag to Arnulf, sitting in the front seat next to him.

Arnulf nodded.

"What is it?" Dag asked.

"I don't know," Arnulf replied.

They both looked around. The full moon's reflection on the Black Forest made every tree and bush appear ghostly and haunted. Dag glanced back at the colonel. Even with only the moonlight to see by, Colonel Strauss could detect the look of fear in the private's eyes. Although he was just as unsettled by the sound as the young soldier, he didn't want to show it and quickly dismissed the noise.

"It's nothing more than a howling wolf," said Strauss. "Drive on," he commanded with a flip of his hand.

Dag shook his head. "That sounds nothing like any wolf I've ever heard," Dag mumbled as he turned the key in the ignition. He was revving up the motor and was about to hit the gas when Adok jumped up from the back seat in a frenzy, knocking the prison skullcap off Hans' head.

"There he is! I see him running there!" shouted Adok, pointing in the direction of the castle to the right of the jeep. The medieval castle was perched high on a bluff. A view of the castle tower and the moon hovering above it could still be seen from over twenty miles away.

"He's running directly towards us."

"Who, Adok?" asked Dr. Weiss.

"A big hairy, bare-chested dark man with a beard and mustache," replied Adok. "He's running fast, and he's carrying something over his shoulder."

"The Schwarze soldat, you mean? Mein Got!" shouted Dr. Weiss.

Colonel Strauss and the doctor glanced at each other in astonishment.

"Where is he? I don't see him," shouted both Dag and Arnulf. The two beamed their flashlights in the direction Adok was pointing.

Everyone in the jeep stood and peered into the woods, trying to discern the shadows in the night. Colonel Strauss pointed his flashlight in one direction, then the other. But not even the full moon's brightness or man-made devices revealed to the colonel and the others what Adok Makowski saw. The boy saw not yards away, but miles away, with the depth and perception of the first successful Nordic superhuman of his race.

"He's going to catch up to us," shouted Adok. "He's running faster!"

"Drive on quickly! Move it!" yelled Strauss.

Before the rest of them could sit down, Dag rammed the gas pedal to the floor and took off, causing them all to fall back into their seats.

All night, Adok informed them of the black soldier's whereabouts as he sat on his knees, leaning against the backseat and looking behind them. He's crossing a bridge; he's running through the streets of a city; he's leaping over a riverbed.

"How can you see him so clearly in the dark?" asked Arnulf.

"Yea?" Dag chimed in, glancing at Adok in his rearview mirror.

Adok turned his head and replied: "I can't see him that clearly in the dark. His image is hazy. But I can still tell how he looks. When he's running fast, I see only a blur of him."

"Turn around all the way in your seat now, Adok. We've heard enough," said Dr. Weiss. "We'll reach Switzerland just before daybreak if we stay on this road. I have a cottage in the small, remote town of Basel. We'll be safe there. No one will ever find us," said Dr. Weiss to Colonel Strauss.

Strauss never replied, but hours later, as soon as there was a glimmer of daylight, he ordered Dag to stop the jeep.

Dag hit the brakes. Strauss got out of the vehicle. "Why are we stopping here? The Swiss border is only ten miles away, and my place is another eleven," said Dr. Weiss.

The colonel ignored the doctor and looked at Arnulf. "Take your binoculars, climb that tree as high as you can, and see if you can see if that Negro soldier is still following us," said Strauss, pointing to the tallest tree alongside the road.

Arnulf obeyed. He climbed but slipped when his left foot touched the third branch. His second attempt resulted in the same outcome.

"He's climbing up the wrong side. Let me try. I can do it! Let me do it!" said Adok eagerly. Colonel Strauss glanced over at Dr. Weiss, who nodded his approval.

"Okay, Arnulf, give him your binoculars," said Strauss.

Adok laughed and shooed Arnulf's hand away. "I don't need those. I've got 20-20 vision.

The professor told me that the seru…."

"Adok! Hurry up and climb that tree. We don't have all morning," interrupted Dr. Weiss.

Adok went to the pine and walked around it once, examining its branches before ascending on the side opposite the road. He scurried up the tree, circling the trunk like he was climbing a winding staircase.

Moving with agility and speed, he took only sixty seconds to reach the top.

"Wow! Look at him go," shouted Dag.

"No human can climb like that!" said Arnulf. Colonel Strauss just watched. He glanced over at Dr. Weiss, looking at his watch. *He's timing the boy. Hmmm.*

CHAPTER SIXTEEN

I, too, sing America. I am the darker brother.
They send me to eat in the kitchen when company
comes, But I laugh, and eat well, and grow strong.
Tomorrow, I'll be at the table when company comes.
Nobody will say to me, "Eat in the kitchen," then.

Besides, they'll see how beautiful I am and be
ashamed— I, too, am America.

Langston Hughes

Once again, Kapp ran through the forest with the moon at his back. This time, he carried the bundled corpse of his stepbrother across his shoulder. His brother's body should have been heavy, but it wasn't. For Kapp, the weight was as light as carrying a football. Kapp had always been strong and stocky. His physique was stout. But now, the muscles rippling across his upper body and down his legs were as hard as chiseled stone.

Kapp had always been a fast runner and a high jumper, too. He once considered joining the track team in college. But Kapp loved football more. Now, every time he put one foot down and lifted the other, he ran with incredible speed. When he jumped over a ditch or a large rock, he catapulted through the air and landed 120 yards away--the length of a football field. Kapp quickly came to a two-lane highway and stopped. He noticed something lying at his feet and picked it up. It was a cap. The dingy, blue, and white striped skullcap was still warm from body heat. Whoever the hat belonged to rode by here not too long ago. Kapp stared at the cap in his hand a little longer and remembered that he'd seen it before on the head of the young man in the castle tower, the one wearing the raggedy prison uniform.

Kapp stuffed the cap into his pants pocket and then gazed down the highway in one direction, then the other. The Nazi colonel and the doctor had gotten away. Again, Kapp glanced down the road in one direction and then the other. He wondered which way they went. He was determined to catch them.

South directed the voice inside his head. Kapp obeyed and walked. He soon trotted, then ran fast, then ran faster—zoom!

CHAPTER SEVENTEEN

Belief is the death of intelligence.

Robert Anton Wilson

Daybreak, May 1, 1945
Basel, Switzerland

Colonel Otto Strauss had never been to Switzerland. The gradual emergence of daylight brought into focus the exquisite beauty of the Swiss countryside. Everywhere Otto looked, there was a picturesque view of rolling green hills and lush valleys set against towering, majestic mountains. If ever there was a place on earth called paradise, this was it, he thought.

Dr. Weiss directed Dag to take the dirt road to the right. Trees lined both sides of the narrow road for a quarter-mile before they reached a clearing. Once they did, the view was breathtaking. Nestled at the bottom, between two sloping hills, was a white brick cottage with a slanting roof surrounded by a meadow of yellow wildflowers. Light blue shutters accented the glass casement windows, a feature of tiny rural houses built in the Eighteenth Century. Behind the cottage lay a forest of luxuriant green trees as far as the eye could see.

Everyone exited the jeep and stood in front of the cottage momentarily, admiring the scenery. Otto ordered Dag and Arnulf to stay outside and stand guard. The décor inside the cabin was warm and cozy. An oversized dark brown herringbone sofa sat facing a stone fireplace adorned with a wide beamed oak mantel. Two slope-backed cowhide armchairs flanked the couch on both sides, with a wooden coffee table in the middle. On the floor was a thick, crème and brown area rug. Otto sat in one chair and watched Hans carry the boy, now fast asleep, up the wooden plank steps to a bedroom with Dr. Weiss leading the way.

"He'll sleep until the afternoon at least," Dr. Weiss informed Otto upon returning downstairs thirty minutes later.

"My nephew will stay in the room just in case the boy happens to wake up."

Dr. Weiss sat down in the other chair across from the colonel. Otto merely nodded his head and remained silent. Neither of them spoke for at least forty minutes.

Otto was replaying in his head everything that had happened since the boy had awakened, notably what occurred just before they arrived at the cottage at daybreak:

The boy can see exceptionally far with merely his bare eyes and without binoculars; how can that be? It's impossible. First, the boy saw the Schwarze soldat running towards us in the woods. We had to be at least ten—no fifteen, at least twenty-five miles away by that time. No human can physically catch up to a vehicle going eighty to one hundred miles per hour on foot and running barefoot at that--impossible! Then, as we traveled west, no south, no southwest towards Switzerland, the boy claims to see the Schwarze soldat running through the streets of Wurttemberg. That must be about, let me see, sixteen, seventeen, or maybe eighteen miles east, uh, no, west of the castle, making it a total distance of over forty-three or something miles. That's incredible for the boy to see. Yet the lad described the buildings in Wurttemberg with such detail, like the store on the corner of Hanover Street, with the red door and the pine wreath hanging on it. It had the black shingle swinging on one hinge and read: Kruger's Tailor Shop.

But the most fantastic thing occurred at the first glint of daybreak when I ordered to stop the jeep and handed my binoculars to Arnulf. Within a blink, the boy looked down at us from the very top of the tree. That pine had to be at least, what, thirty-feet tall? But the boy scurried up the tree trunk with the quickness of a squirrel. We all looked up at him in awe with our mouths open, except Dr. Weiss. He didn't seem surprised by Adok's ability to climb like that. I caught him glancing at his watch as if timing the boy to see how fast the child could reach the top. Then, as soon as the doctor noticed me watching him, he tried to appear surprised. The doctor yelled at Adok to tell us what he saw. Adok was shouting down at us, but he was so high up that the only words we could hear were, "Zoom! Zoom!"

I finally motioned for the boy to come down.

"He's jumped clear across the Danube River and is running through the Kreuztor Gate," Adok said excitedly when he climbed down from the tree.

The Kreuztor Gate was in Ingolstadt, at least a hundred miles from Switzerland. He's heading towards Austria. How could the black soldier run so far, so fast?

More importantly, Ingolstadt was only thirty-four miles away from our military stronghold in Regensburg. If the boy could see that far, the serum must do much more than enable one to live forever. There can be no other explanation for the boy and the Schwarze soldat performing such amazing feats. Oh, yes, and I forgot about him climbing the tower wall. I thought he was crazy. The doctor knew he wasn't. He's known all along. But why didn't the doctor tell me about these abilities before? If the serum gives you such abilities, why is Dr. Weiss keeping it a secret? What is his purpose for doing so, and what else is he hiding from me?

He doesn't trust me. What other reason can there be for not telling me? But why doesn't he trust me? I've done nothing to warrant his mistrust. Still, he doesn't have faith in me. Now that I think back on it, I recall what the doctor said when he showed me how the antidote worked. He said, "You don't think I would create a serum that gives humans the ability to overcome death without creating an antidote, do you? For every great man who rises to power, there are two or three lesser men like you who think they are just as great waiting in the wings to overthrow him." Like me, he said. Hmmm! Well, trust me or not, my dear

Dr. Weiss, you will inject my two soldiers and me with the serum. You must, and you will!

Otto rose from his chair and straightened his uniform. He stood for several seconds with his shoulders arched back and his chest out, which accentuated his height and gave him a more commanding presence. He then peered down at the doctor, still seated.

"We must talk, Dr. Weiss," he finally spoke. His voice was loud and dictatorial, a tone befitting someone with the high rank of an Oberstfuhrer.

"Yes, I know," acknowledged the doctor. "Come this way." Dr. Weiss leads the Oberstfuhrer past the dining room, through the kitchen, out the back door, and across a neglected vegetable garden into the woods. Strauss wondered where the doctor was taking him. Just beyond some pine trees was a small wooden storage shed. The two entered.

"Here, help me move this work table," insisted the doctor.

Otto picked up one end of the table as Dr. Weiss picked up the other. The two moved it to one side. Dr. Weiss removed a dirty coverlet from the floor to reveal a trap door.

"This way, Kommandant," directed Dr. Weiss as he lifted the door and led the way down the wooden stairs. The doctor flicked on the light switch to reveal three rolls of laboratory tables placed next to each other horizontally in the center of the room. Bunsen burners, Erlenmeyer flasks, beakers, glass test tubes, and whatever else was needed to conduct experiments cluttered the table. Wooden bookshelves lined the walls with medical and scientific books and stacks of handwritten notes and papers.

Otto walked about the room while the doctor stood by the steps.

"Is there something you're not telling me, doctor, something about the serum?"

Like what?" Dr. Weiss asked.

"Come, come now, doctor. You must have noticed how the boy climbed that tree. He ran up the tree as quickly as a squirrel. And what about his sight-- the distance he's able to see? Then there's the running ability of the Negro soldier. Did the serum give them these abilities?"

Dr. Weiss hesitated. "Yes," he finally admitted. "An unexpected but amazing side effect of the serum is that it greatly enhances whatever skills you naturally excel at or possess. Adok, who loves to climb and has a natural ability, can now climb like a squirrel, as you say. Because he was born with 20/20 vision, his eyesight surpasses even that of an eagle who can see hundreds of miles away."

Excited by the doctor's revelations, Otto walked over to Dr. Weiss and embraced him, placing his hands on the doctor's shoulders.

"You will give the serum to my men and me. It should be today, tonight!" Otto proclaimed. "We must not waste any more time."

Dr. Weiss turned aside and walked over to the nearest laboratory table.

"I have no intention of injecting you with the serum, Kommandant," uttered Dr. Weiss in a firm and resolute voice. Otto felt the muscles in his neck tighten.

"Wha-what do you mean?" He stuttered with a strained and shaky voice.

"I mean, Kommandant, that you are not a good candidate for the serum. There are no unique characteristics or abilities that you excel at that would be enhanced if you received the serum."

"That's not true! I am a good candidate! I am! What I excel at is simple. I excel at being German, and as a German, I am a member of the master race, just like you, just like the Fuhrer. So how can you make such a judgment against me?"

"How, you say? In the same way, we make judgments against the Jews and Negros, even against others of our race who don't possess the ideal Aryan features of blonde hair and blue eyes.

Have we not set these physical attributes as the standard for determining who is of pure blood and who is not? Without such criteria, how can one race claim to be master over another? Doesn't every race naturally believe their race is better than all others? But mere belief is not enough. We must have standards and rules, draw boundaries, and set limits, or the claim of our superiority is without merit.

Before I knew the serum could enhance one's natural abilities, I was content with the prospect of Germans just living forever as the symbol of our supremacy. Now, I realized that my thinking was too small-minded. It should have been the purpose of the serum all along to give certain Germans not only extraordinarily long lives but also to make them physically superior.

Throughout the centuries, great men of science have labored to invent a substance that would produce endless life. The "Elixir of Life" is what they called it. Now, I, a lowly German physician my colleagues once denounced as crazy, have succeeded where all others have failed. And, as its sole creator, I have the absolute right to determine who shall partake of it and who shall not, and I have determined, Kommandant, that you shall not partake of it."

Otto stood silently as the doctor spoke. The doctor's words were like daggers plunging into his back, slitting his spine from pillar to post. Otto couldn't move. There was paralysis in every muscle and joint in his body. He couldn't speak or even pucker his lips. It was as if his mouth had been wired shut. Worse was his inability to think or articulate a coherent thought in response to the doctor's objections.

The rats were biting again, and the voice inside Otto's head kept shouting repeatedly. Kill the rats! The same voice responded. Yes, kill the rat!

"Your height is the only positive attribute you possess. While being six feet four inches tall is desirable, it doesn't compare with overpowering brute strength or the ability to climb like a squirrel or see farther than an eagle. You are an average man with average intelligence, possessing less-than-average physical abilities.

Not to mention, you have a decidedly unappealing face--certainly not the Aryan ideal. It would be pointless and a waste of the serum to administer it to you. It takes nearly six months to make just thirty-two fluid ounces of the liquid. One injection requires four ounces. I have only twelve vials left, having accidentally given one to that American Negro soldier. I won't waste another." Weiss shook his head.

"No, I'm sorry, Kommandant, you will not do! You simply will not do. However, the two young soldiers under your command might be good candidates, especially the youngest one, Dag. He has quick reflexes. I can tell that by the way he drives. He may possess other abilities as well. I don't know about the other one, Arnulf. I will have to examine both of them further. But it will be time enough for that after breakfast. A couple of slices of Brötchen bread and marmalade with some Gouda cheese, sausage, and fresh hot ground coffee will do us all some good," said the doctor in a lighter tone as he walked to the stairs. The doctor climbed several steps before looking back at Otto, who was still frozen in the same spot.

"Are you coming, Kommandant?"

Otto's eyes blinked rapidly. Focus, he told himself. A thousand thoughts were swimming in his head, and he couldn't make sense of any of them. His brain felt as though it had been split apart, and large buckets of muddy water were pouring into the opening. He felt dejected and overwhelmed, helpless and useless. Dr. Weiss called out to him again. Finally, Otto gave in and followed Dr. Weiss up the steps and out of the shed.

He walked several paces behind the doctor, clutching his right arm as if in pain. He trudged back to the cottage, his head hung down, pouting and teary-eyed.

CHAPTER EIGHTEEN

We took bridges, we took towns…and
the Germans respected us.
They called us Schwarze Soldaten (black soldiers).
The word had passed back through
Germany that these black soldiers were coming,
and they were afraid.

E.G., McConnell 761st Tank Battalion

Noon, May 1, 1945
Bavaria

For Lieutenant Milton Taylor, nothing was as dangerous in war as silence. Taylor was one of the first black officers assigned to the 761st Tank Battalion, and his military training taught him to treat silence like an all-out enemy attack. That's why his nerves felt like needles as C Company marched in column formation down a narrow road outside the ancient city of Straubing. The 761st Tank Battalion and his military training taught him to treat silence like an all-out enemy attack. That's why his nerves felt like needles as C Company marched in column formation down a narrow road outside the ancient city of Straubing. The 761st spearheaded the drive to Austria for the Third Army's 71st Infantry Division under General Patton and the 12th Army Group. Lieutenant Taylor rode in the lead tank. As he peered out over the commander's hatch of his M4 Sherman, he couldn't help but feel as though the whole world had stopped breathing.

There was no sound of sparrows chirping or leaves rustling in the wind. There was no wind or visible signs of life in any direction he could see. The air was stiff, and the earth was still.

Somewhere between here and Austria, the lieutenant knew the Germans were poised to attack again with whatever they had left. Common sense told him there was no way the Nazis would allow the Americans to join up with the Russians, which would signal the end of the war. Eight days ago, they had taken in a hard-fought battle, the port town of Regensburg, a critical military base at the hub of a network of highways that connected many of the Army's essential operations in northeast Germany. South of Regensburg was Austria, the final destination. Three days ago, they liberated the Dachau concentration camp. The horrors Lieutenant Taylor saw there were seared into his mind forever. Since then, the Third Army and an attachment of the 761st had encountered just a few pockets of die-hard Wehrmacht determined to fight for the Fatherland to the death. One or two hours of combat were usually all it took to drive the Jerries into retreat and capture the town. But the unit's campaign through Bavaria was uneventful. In every city and rural village, friendly burghers greeted them, waving the white flags of surrender from their doorposts and windows. As they plowed closer to Austria, they encountered large, wandering bands of newly freed prisoners crawling along the highways. It was a tragic sight to see humans so starved they looked dead than alive and only walking skeletons.

Now, with seventy-five more miles to go before they reached the bank of the Enns River to cross over into Austria, no bedraggled, emaciated prisoners of war had passed along this highway for several hours. Everything was quiet, too quiet, which was why instincts told Lieutenant Taylor to be wary. He was right. A shell came out of nowhere as their convoy came to a grove of trees alongside the road.

Boom! The air crackled and hissed. Lieutenant Taylor suddenly found himself engulfed in smoke and choking on gasoline fumes. A shell had hit his tank. Through the flames, he could see the gruesome remains of his four-man tank crew lying on the road. Boom! Boom! A steady barrage of shellfire blasted through the trees. Bolts of fire from blown-up tanks erupted behind him. Exploding shells crisscrossed the air, halting the procession. Severed pieces of body parts, along with seared bits of tree bark, went hurling through the sky as the moans, cries, and screams from the injured and dying filled his ears. Around him was chaos. Officers were shouting orders as soldiers ran for cover.

Lieutenant Taylor quickly got on his horn to radio their location for air support. All he got was static. His two-way communication had been knocked out.

"Get outta there, Taylor!" yelled Colonel Baker.

Taylor heard the colonel and tried to lift himself out of the hatch but couldn't. The slightest movement sent jolts of sharp, piercing pain rippling through his chest. Taylor was bleeding on the left side of his body from a piece of shrapnel lodged just below his rib cage. He knew it was all over for him.

The heat from the Sherman was like a furnace. Charlie Company was getting pummeled, and he was stuck in a burning tank, soon to be consumed by fire or blasted again by another shell. There was nothing he could do now but pray. The flames were spreading up from the front of the hull and getting closer to the commander's hatch. Burning to death was a horrible way to die, he thought.

Taylor closed his eyes and lowered his head. "The Lord is my Sheppard, I…"

A sudden and loud thump interrupted him. He opened his eyes.

At first, he didn't know what he was seeing. Something or someone appeared to move towards him on the hull. It was hard to see through the curls of white and gray smoke and spits of fire. He heard what sounded like a cough, and the next thing he knew, someone stepped through the burning blaze. Lieutenant Taylor looked up and saw a ghost. He couldn't believe his eyes. Standing before him, stout and sturdy, bare-chested and bigger than life, was a soldier from C Company he listed as Killed in Action three months ago.

"Sergeant Johnson, my God, is that you!?"

CHAPTER NINETEEN

"Out of every, one hundred men, ten shouldn't
even be there,
eighty are just targets; nine are the real fighters,
and we are lucky to have them, for they make
the battle.
Ah, but the one, one is a warrior, and he will
bring the others back."

Heraclitus

Noon, May 1, 1945

Kapp didn't even feel his feet touch the ground as he ran. It was as if he was running on air. The scenery around him was a blur as Kapp raced across the countryside. How fast he was running, he didn't know, as quickly as the fastest automobile. It didn't feel like he was running, merely jogging. His heartbeat was slow and steady. His legs were strong and nimble.

He never felt tired and had no desire to eat. He stopped only to relieve himself.

He ran all night before he came to a long, winding riverbank just before daybreak. He jumped the entire length of the river in one soaring leap without breaking his stride and while still carrying the body of his dead stepbrother across his shoulders. He kept on running. He ran through an ancient stone archway and the empty medieval streets of an unknown Bavarian town, the inhabitants still asleep.

He continued running for miles through valleys, rocky riverbeds, and open farmland. It wasn't until he stopped to relieve himself in the woods for the first time around midday he heard the familiar sound of mortar and artillery fire coming from somewhere north of his location. The Germans were fighting Russians or fighting Americans. Either way, he would meet up with them; the sooner, the better. He quickly finished his business, slung his brother's body over his shoulders, and ran toward the bombing. He quickly caught up to the fighting.

Kapp spotted the battle in progress as he cleared the woods. Standing on a high hill, he looked down at the scene to his left, about three hundred yards away. It was a U. S. Army division, all right. He could spot a Sherman from almost any distance. One could hardly call it a battle. It was more like a slaughter. The Americans were getting carpet-bombed with a constant barrage of heavy artillery directed from behind a large grove of trees on the opposite side of the highway. The road was cluttered with seven abandoned, disabled, and destroyed armored vehicles. About fifteen or so dead soldiers lay scattered on the road like litter. The rest of the unit took cover in a deep ravine across the street, a yard away from their convoy.

Kapp remembered the last time he and his stepbrother fought with their unit, Charlie Company. It was earlier this year, on January 5th, during a long, grueling battle in Tillet, France. Pauli was a gunner and a member of Kapp's tank crew. No one knew they were stepbrothers, or they could never have served in the same battalion together, much less manned the same tank.

Charlie Company had been assigned to give armor support to the 26th Infantry Division, an all-white unit nicknamed the "Yankee Division" because all the soldiers hailed from Northeastern states. His tank crew was roaring up a hill and had taken out several pillboxes along the way when a mine blast disabled his Sherman. Kapp ordered his crew to abandon ship. The entire team escaped and was running down the hill for cover when a grenade exploded thirty feet in front of his stepbrother, causing Pauli to change directions. Scared and confused, his brother ran back up the slope toward the German firing line.

"Come back, Pauli! Come back!" Kapp yelled, but Pauli didn't stop. Kapp had always been fast enough to chase down his brother. Not this time. Pauli reached the hilltop and disappeared over the other side. Kapp ran after him and suddenly found himself surrounded by Jerries. He surrendered, raised his hands behind his head, and kneeled next to his stepbrother. Kapp expected a bullet in both their heads. What he felt was a hard blow to the back of his skull, then everything went black.

He woke up beside Pauli on the floor of a truck. Kapp never understood why the Germans didn't kill both. The Germans fed them a decent ration of sausage, beans, and bread. For months, the Jerries moved them from place to place until they finally ended up in the castle dungeon three days ago.

Kapp carefully laid his brother's body down on the hill where he stood. It was time to rejoin the war. Backing up about sixty paces, he ran to the farthest edge of the slope and leaped a hundred and twenty yards through the air. As soon as his feet touched the ground, he was running. Kapp ran so fast that it was hard to see where he was going. He was barely breathing. His body felt loose and relaxed. He slowed down to a trot to check his location. Immediately, his eyes were drawn to the lead tank on the road. He spotted a soldier's head sticking out of the commander's hatch.

He must be pinned in.

Kapp knew that the tank would blow any minute. He caught sight of a large boulder three feet high and sixty feet away. He built up speed and used the rock as a springboard to catapult himself through the air over the ravine and onto the tank.

He landed right into the flames on the front hull of the Sherman. Both his pants legs caught on fire. The heat was intense, but it didn't bother him. Kapp coughed, overwhelmed by the fumes as he walked towards the commander's hatch. He passed through a cloud of smoke and suddenly stood before the tank commander.

"Sergeant Johnson, my God, is that you!? Where the hell did you come from?"

"From the other side of hell," Kapp replied, now recognizing Lieutenant Taylor.

"But it will be time enough to talk about that later, lieutenant, because the hell we're in now is about to explode."

Kapp grabbed Taylor under the officer's right arm and lifted him out of the hatch with one hand. He flung the lieutenant over his shoulder, leaped off the tank, and landed in the ravine.

As Kapp's feet touched the ground, the Sherman blew up, filling the sky with more smoke. The vibrations from the blast resonated through the air like a thousand clashing cymbals. It was loud enough to rattle bones and burst eardrums. Medics and stretcher barriers rushed over to assist Kapp with Lieutenant Taylor.

Most of the soldiers, including Colonel Baker, huddled together in the ravine as the medics gently laid the lieutenant on the stretcher. No one was paying attention to the bombing for the moment. The twelve-foot-deep gully gave the unit some cover. Everyone had their eyes fixed on Kapp.

A halo of white smoke surrounded his body. His bushy, dark brown hair had grown three inches high and resembled a big clump of wool. A thick, coarse beard concealed his cheeks and chin. His mustache, beard, and hairline converged into one dense mass of hair framing his face.

"Look who's come back from the dead, Sergeant Johnson," announced Lieutenant Taylor to Colonel Baker as the medics attended to the lieutenant's wounds. At first, the colonel didn't reply. He just stared in disbelief. Kapp noticed the colonel's apprehension and straightened his posture. He pulled back his shoulders stuck out his bare chest and then raised his right hand in salute.

"Sergeant Kapp Johnson, United States Army 761st Tank Battalion, Charlie Company, reporting for duty, sir."

"Where have you been, son?" asked Colonel Baker. Before Kapp could account for his whereabouts, a shell exploded overhead, and shrapnel rained down upon them. Colonel Baker sustained a shoulder wound. Others weren't as lucky. One medic attending Lieutenant Taylor died instantly. He had just wrapped a bandage around the lieutenant's chest when shrapnel blasted several holes in his skull. Bits of the medic's brain spurted out of the top of his head. What remained of the rest of him collapsed on top of Lieutenant Taylor, shielding the lieutenant from being hit a second time. It was a horrific sight, and equally dreadful were the tortured cries of soldiers screaming, "Oh God, Mama, and help me, Jesus."

Everywhere Kapp looked was a gory, bloody mess of shredded and mutilated flesh scattered like manure on the ground. He had also been hit. Shrapnel struck him in the neck, temporarily blocking his air passage. Gasping for breath, Kapp grabbed his throat and inhaled. A second later, he removed his hand and held a small piece of shrapnel in his palm. Kapp slipped the metal piece into his pants pocket just before hundreds of Germans swarmed over the embankment into the ravine.

Suddenly, the air was filled with the spat and rata-tat-tat of rifle and machine-gun fire. Every uninjured and wounded American soldier able to fight engaged the Jerries in hand-to-hand combat. Once again, Kapp's blood grew hot, and he felt invincible. His heartbeat raced. The ligaments surrounding his muscles expanded, causing his reflexes to react at lightning-quick speed. He quickly pounded the Jerries into the ground. He split their skulls with one hammer-like thump on the top of their heads with his fists. He snatched their weapons out of their hands and splattered the Nazi soldiers to pieces with their rifles and machine guns. In twenty minutes, Sergeant Johnson singlehandedly killed two hundred and eighty German Soldiers.

American air support finally arrived and bombed the hell out of the German Tiger tanks docked behind the now obliterated grove of trees on the other side of the road. The fighting was over. The Americans won.

CHAPTER TWENTY

Whoever undertakes to set himself up as a
judge
of Truth
and Knowledge is
shipwrecked by the laughter of
the gods.

Albert Einstein

2:00 PM, MAY 1, 1945
Basel, Switzerland

"Do you want to kill me, Kommandant? I know you do. I can see it in your eyes."

Josef Olaf Weiss had always been a man of direct words and decisive actions, and even more so now at seventy-eight. He didn't mince words or dance around the edges of the truth. He wasn't impressed with Kommandant Strauss and told him so when the colonel arrived five days ago.

"Why did they send you to me? What qualifications do you have? Are you a scientist or a doctor? Have you ever studied at a university?"

"I'm a colonel in the German Army and a full-fledged member of the Nazi Party, and that's all you need to know," was the response Colonel Strauss gave. But that wasn't good enough for the doctor. Josef Weiss was a self-assuming, arrogant man who couldn't abide being with men of elementary intellect, Nazi Party members or not.

"You're an ugly man. I don't like you and don't want you here," said the doctor.

Only after Weiss read the letter of introduction Hitler signed, did his attitude toward the colonel change. In the letter, the Fuhrer first apologized for sending Strauss, acknowledging that the colonel was not the caliber of soldier commissioned for such a task if events in the war hadn't demanded that Hitler's best and most trusted advisors remained at his side. Hitler explained that Strauss' promotion to the rank of colonel was solely to make Strauss more acceptable to report on the progress of the doctor's experiments. Weiss could believe that. The war wasn't going well. For the first time since its start, whispers of a German defeat were spreading through the Reich. In July, Hitler barely escaped an attempt on his life inside his Wolf's Lair Field Headquarters near Rastenburg in East Prussia. Weiss didn't like it, but if Strauss was the best man, the Fuhrer could send. He had no choice but to accept him.

"Did you read this letter Kommandant?"

"Of course not!" Colonel Strauss refuted strongly.

"No, you wouldn't have, and there's no need to get testy. Perhaps I've misjudged you. Maybe I should have read the letter first before assessing your qualifications. I apologize. Come this way, and I will show you my progress. I think the Fuhrer will be very pleased."

That combustive first meeting was just last week. How quickly things had changed. Now, Hitler was dead. Germany had lost the war, and the doctor's dreams of creating a master race may never become a reality. Weiss wished he had taken the Fuhrer's advice a year ago and let other scientists assist him with his experiments, but he wouldn't hear of it. Weiss didn't want to share his glory with doctors who had once called him a kook and a friend. The medical board suspended his license to practice medicine. In his eyes, none were good enough to breathe the same air as him, much less work side-by-side with him. Until she died in 1943, only his young wife, Gitta, was worthy of assisting him.

Gitta Bergen had been a brilliant physicist and had become as obsessed with the serum as he, unlike Olga, his first wife, who disapproved of his experiments and had divorced him twenty years prior because of it. Weiss met Gitta at the University of Munich when he came to give a lecture to her biophysics class. She was twenty-two years old when they married. He was old enough to be her grandfather. Gitta didn't care. She proposed to him. At first, he didn't take her proposal seriously. He thought it was nothing more than a young girl's infatuation. After months of turning her down, she finally persuaded him to marry her. One evening, in tears, Gitta declared her undying love and devotion to him.

"A brilliant mind is what makes a man young and powerful," declared Gitta affectionately. "And that makes you, darling, the youngest and most powerful man I am ever likely to meet in my lifetime."

They wed on September 22, 1939. Weiss remembered how she wore her long, silky blonde hair up in a bun to make herself look older and more sophisticated. At that very moment, Weiss could smell the sweet scent of his wife's Edelweiss perfume. He touched his lips, remembering the softness of her rosy-pink lips pressed against his. His marriage to Gitta was the happiest years of his life. Tragically, it didn't last long.

Stop it! His mind shouted. Weiss shook his head repeatedly to shake his memories away. *You must focus on the present. Gitta's dead.*

Re-focusing his attention, Weiss again glanced over at Kommandant Strauss. The colonel stood in the doorway of the downstairs utility room, where the doctor was about to administer the serum to the two young soldiers. The Kommandant stood there stark and still like a pouting adolescent, with his fists tightly balled, looking on as the doctor tied Arnulf and Dag securely to the makeshift cots with black leather straps. A seething look of resentment colored the colonel's pimple-red face. It made the doctor nervous. Earlier that day, he had brushed away repeated pleas by the Kommandant to inject him with the serum. Now, the colonel had to endure watching the two young soldiers under his command receive what he coveted for himself. Weiss knew enough about human nature to be cautious when dealing with an angry, jealous man--particularly one of low intelligence. He wanted to hurry up with the injections and remove himself from the Kommandant's presence.

Weiss had given the two soldiers a drug to put them to sleep and was waiting until they were under before injecting them with the serum. Arnulf had fallen off several minutes ago, but young Dag was still fading in and out of consciousness.

"Stop fighting the drug and close your eyes. If you don't fall asleep, I won't inject you with the serum. You won't become like Adok and possess extraordinary abilities. Remember what I said would happen to you; because you are double-jointed, you can bend your body into the shape of a pretzel or collapse your chest and fold it in half. You would like to be able to do that, wouldn't you? But without the serum, you will remain just an ordinary boy," said Dr. Weiss. "Do you want to be just an ordinary person for the rest of your life?"

Dag shook his head from side-to-side.

"Then close your eyes and keep them closed." Dag obeyed and fell fast asleep within seconds.

Weiss leaned over to check Dag's pulse before walking over to the other cot to check Arnulf's. Both heartbeats were slow and steady. Good. It was time. Dr. Weiss moved over to the round table positioned between the two cots. On top of the table was the doctor's large alabaster case lined in red velvet, containing twenty-seven vials of pale red and pinkish-red liquid. Eleven of the four-ounce glass tubes contained the serum. The other fifteen included the deadly hallucinogenic drug that killed the young Negro soldier. He purposely put the drug and the elixir in the same case to make it even harder for the Kommandant to determine which vials contained the Elixir of Life.

The doctor knew his invention. He knew how the serum looked and smelled and even the speed at which it flowed from the syringe when injected into the body. He would not get nervous and mistake one for the other this time.

With his back to the colonel, Weiss opened the case. He grabbed two of the vials and immediately filled the syringe. But he almost dropped the needle when he suddenly felt the Kommandant's hot, stinky breath on the nape of his neck. Strauss was standing so close behind the doctor that less than an inch of space separated the two.

"Mein Got! You idiot! Stand back! You almost made me drop the serum!" Dr. Weiss shot a stern glance over his shoulder, hoping it would cause the colonel to back away. Instead, the doctor felt pain in his stomach as the colonel's body pressed against the doctor, pinning Weiss against the oak table.

The Kommandant's tall frame squeezed against Dr. Weiss's frail body, making him feel vulnerable and afraid. To calm his nerves, Weiss inhaled quickly and slowly exhaled.

"Will you please step back, Kommandant?" This time, the inflection in the doctor's voice was conciliatory and kind. But that didn't work either.

Strauss gripped the shoulders of Dr. Weiss. The doctor's body stiffened. The colonel's hands were heavy and felt like the weight of two iron barbells bearing down on him.

"Release me, you fool! What do you think you're doing!?" Dr. Weiss screamed as he wiggled his body, trying to break free. But the more Dr. Weiss struggled, the harder the colonel bore down.

Pressing his dry, chapped lips against the doctor's ear, the Kommandant whispered: "Tell me your name and the name of your commanding officer?"

Dr. Weiss froze. The steely, deep-throated tone of the colonel's voice sounded so evil, so sinister; only the voice of the devil himself could have sounded as wicked, Weiss thought.

The colonel is not the devil; he's just a low-class bully, an imbecile in want of power.

Weiss cleared his throat and tried to regain his composure.

"I will allow you to inject yourself with the serum after I have injected Dag and Arnulf. You don't have any objections to the two of them taking the serum, do you?"

"No," said the colonel.

"Good. Then, after I inject your soldiers, if you can figure out which of the remaining vials contains the serum, that vial will be yours."

The Kommandant let out a half-hearted chuckle.

Weiss winced as the colonel's hands slid from his shoulders up to his neck without the colonel loosening his grip.

"No! Give me the syringe in your hand."

"Yes, of course," Dr. Weiss quickly obeyed, extending his right arm back to the Kommandant.

Dr. Weiss saw Strauss reach for the needle out of the corner of his eye. Just as Strauss was about to grab it, Dr. Weiss opened his hand and let the syringe slip from his fingers. The glass syringe broke into pieces on the table, with some liquid spilling on the floor.

The colonel gasped, and immediately let go of the doctor's neck.

Free, Dr. Weiss quickly walked around to the other side of the table. The colonel looked at Strauss in disbelief, standing motionless, staring down at the splattered liquid.

Dr. Weiss grinned.

"Did you think I was going to let you take by force what has taken me most of my life to create and cost me the lives of my beloved wife and son? Did you truly think that I was going to hand over my creation to you just because you threatened me with death? What is death to a man who won't live out the month?"

A look of confusion flashed across the Kommandant's face.

Dr. Weiss continued.

"Yes, you heard me right. There is a great irony to my life that you are unaware of Kommandant. I am dying of cancer and have only weeks or perhaps days to live. You may think the simple solution would be for me to take the serum. But the gods have played a cruel trick on me. Although I am the creator of the Elixir of Life, I cannot partake myself.

You see, long before I injected Adok, I injected my son Olaf with the serum. He was fifteen and a genius, of course. He suggested a slight change in the chemical formula that finally made the serum work. He was as eager as I to test it. Confident it would work, I injected him with the serum without hesitation. It did work, but the result was horrific. In just two days, he woke up from his first death. Ten days later, I gave him cyanide to kill him again. He woke up eight hours later. By the fourth death, his resurrection was literally in a blink of an eye. But over several months, I noticed that his brainpower was increasing enormously. He became obsessed with obtaining knowledge. He learned to speak two hundred languages, including various sign languages, in just two weeks. He read everything in sight, including science books, history books, astronomy, and highly advanced books on quantum mathematics. He was getting smarter by the day, which caused his brain to grow. His cranium swelled to four times its size.

He became so smart he developed a numerical code for speaking, which made him sound like a babbling idiot, not the genius he was. Even in his sleep, He never stopped thinking; he would mumble equations, formulas, facts, and figures. Eventually, his brain was so active he stopped sleeping altogether. He would go for weeks without eating before his body took over, which forced him to take in nourishment. Then he ate everything in sight like a ravenous bull. One day, he was skin and bones. The next day, he was fat and fit. But he hated his existence and prayed to

God to let him die forever. He pleaded with me to kill him for good.

One day he screamed and never stopped. My son just sat in his room and cried, screamed, and hollered as if someone was killing him. All that knowledge had driven him mad. That's when I worked on an antidote to reverse the serum. I succeeded, but not in the way I intended. Once your immune system is enhanced, the only way to change it is to eradicate the immune system, resulting in permanent death.

I had repeatedly given my son cyanide to kill him and speed up the resurrection process. There was no sign of cyanide in his bloodstream when he woke from his many deaths. But once I gave him what I thought to be the antidote, his body showed signs of cyanide poisoning. His skin turned a bright cherry-red and reeked of bitter almonds. That is how the cure became the anti-serum. By that time, my first wife, Olga, had left me. She couldn't bear to see our son that way. She threatened to report me to the police. She never did. However, she did tell the medical board. They revoked my license. I stopped all my experiments after Olaf's death. For years, I hid the formula and did nothing but give lectures at universities and scientific societies. It was at a conference that I met my second wife, Gitta.

Gitta was eighteen and a first-year physics student. She reminded me of Olaf. Like my son, she was intelligent and thirsty for knowledge. We developed a close friendship over the years, which led to marriage. With the growing influence of the Nazi Party and the talk of a New World Order in which Germans would rule supreme over the entire earth; my serum seemed to be the logical answer to the nation's ambitions. My wife encouraged me to experiment with the serum again and wrote a letter explaining it to Hitler.

Together, we worked to find a solution that would inhibit the brain from rapidly increasing its intellectual capacity and alter the deadly effect it had on females. After several years of intense work, we thought we had corrected both problems, but it needed human testing. I wrote to Hitler requesting that I be sent a brainy girl from one of the Lebensborn Homes to test it on, but my dear wife couldn't wait and injected the serum without my knowledge. Three weeks after taking the serum, she was dead. Acute Leukemia took hold, and like my son, her head had swollen enormously."

Weiss blinked his eyes to fight back his tears. "It's not fair; it's not fair. After all I've sacrificed, I get nothing. It's not fair!"

Dr. Weiss reached into his pants pocket, pulled out a handkerchief, and wiped his eyes. Once composed, he used his handkerchief to wipe away the liquid and broken glass from the table.

"Now that you know that those two vials were not filled with the serum of the remaining twenty-five vials, only eleven hold the Elixir of Life. The liquid in each of them looks almost identical. Remember, in a moment of haste, even I couldn't tell them apart and accidentally chose the wrong vial. So, do you think you will be able to do so? Would you like to take a chance and pick one now? Go ahead, choose. If you select the correct vial, you will be resurrected in five or more days or perhaps one or two days if your metabolism works that quickly. If you choose the wrong vial, you will die, and that will be the end of you. However, if you watch me select the serum from the case, allowing me to inject Arnulf and Dag first, you may be able to detect the settled differences in the color and composition and increase your chances of selecting the right one. If you choose the correct one, you will already have three and a half recruits to command once you awaken. I will leave you the formula and the remaining vials of serum."

"Three and a half?" Strauss asked.

"Yes. The boy Adok makes the half, and Dag, Arnulf, and Hans make three. I injected Hans with the serum this morning after he and I put Adok to bed. I strapped him into a chair in Adok's room and tied a scarf over his mouth to muffle his screams. As my brother's only son, at least someone in my family will benefit from my creation. It's only fair."

Weiss reached across the table and pulled the alabaster case towards him. He retrieved another syringe from the side pocket inside the case. "So, shall we begin Kommandant?"

The colonel nodded.

CHAPTER TWENTY-ONE

To preserve a man alive in the midst
of so many chances and hostilities,
is as great a miracle as to create him.

Jeremy Taylor

3:00 PM, May 1, 1945
Bavaria

General Patton's Third Army and the 761st Tank Battalion camped below the hill where Sergeant Johnson laid the burnt corpse of his stepbrother on top of the slope. Kapp looked down from the hill as two medics carried Pauli's body away. Like a colony of ants, the men moved about the camp or stood huddled outside their pup tents.

Usually, after hours of fierce fighting, the last thing soldiers wanted to do was talk. Quiet reflection and silent prayers thanking God for surviving another day of hell were for the moments just after a battle. The only sounds came from the tormented cries and moans of wounded soldiers. Some lay on stretchers. Others lay across blankets spread on the ground, waiting for evacuation to the nearest medical camp. If the wounded were lucky to be given enough morphine to deaden their pain, they lay quietly in a drug-induced stupor. If they were luckier still, the morphine allowed them the blessing of sleep.

For non-wounded soldiers, sleep was a dream deferred. New images of death and destruction, too horrific to contemplate, haunted their minds while awake, only to become even more vivid if they closed their eyes. Gradually, the moments of somber reflection relinquished their hold and gave way to the desire of the human spirit not to become consumed entirely by tragedy but to overcome such terrifying events with jokes, laughter, and a focus on the mundane, everyday pleasures of life.

This time, there was no somber reflection. Everyone in the camp, including the wounded, had been talking nonstop for hours from the time the fighting stopped. The entire camp was abuzz with voices, all unified in their amazement about what occurred on the battlefield that day.

"Sir, I saw something out of the corner of my eye and looked up. This soldier, who turned out to be Sergeant Johnson, was sailing over the ravine," related Colonel Baker to General Patton.

"Suddenly, sir, he just appeared on the hull of my tank as if he had been dropped from heaven," Lieutenant Taylor told the General.

"He killed all those Jerries with his bare hands," declared a white officer in the 71st Infantry to several others in the 12th Army Corps.

"One thump, that's all it took, and every Jerry he hit on the head fell dead," told a wounded tank driver from Charlie Company to a group of fifteen soldiers from the 761st Able Company.

"Captain Carter, it was unbelievable. I saw him get popped at least three or four times. The bullets were bouncing off of him left and right while he just kept on fighting," said Private Ray Wilson, tank cannoneer in Charlie Company.

"I still can't believe what he did, General Patton, sir. He lifted me out of the commander's hatch with one hand like I was nothing more than a toy soldier; he was standing on the tank in his bare feet with both his pants legs on fire."

"What we need to know, sir is where Sergeant Johnson has been all these months and what information the Nazis may have been able to coerce out of him," Colonel Baker said.

"Where is he now?" asked General Patton. "He's getting cleaned up. The unit surgeon,

Captain Carter will give him a physical and will escort him here at 1600 hours," said Colonel Baker, glancing down at his watch, "which is in about an hour from now, sir."

Captain Robert Carter was a short Negro doctor with a round face and a big nose. A native of New York, Carter received his Master of Surgery degree from Howard University Medical School in 1937, where he had the privilege of being instructed by Dr. Charles Drew--the renowned Colored doctor famous for developing the method of processing and preserving blood plasma.

Carter dreamed of becoming a chief surgeon at a city hospital one day and felt that the demands of being an army surgeon put him one step closer to achieving his dream. Nothing he would see at a hospital back home would ever compare to the horrors he saw during the past 29 months. Dr. Carter witnessed what war could do to the human body and bore the sights and smells of obliterated flesh in all its ghastly conditions, from broken, burned, and blasted to shot up, torn up, crushed, and severed. Still, as gruesome as this was, nothing made Captain Carter more afraid of what he saw than now.

"I'm scared for you, son," admitted the captain to Sergeant Johnson.

Kapp sat on the examination table in his underwear, haircut, and clean-shaven. Just minutes before, Captain Carter had taken a scalpel and made a horizontal incision an inch deep across the inner part of Johnson's forearm, only to see the incision close as quickly as Captain Carter made it, leaving no scar. The blood from the cut rapidly dissipated as if it was being sucked back into the sergeant's veins. Carter repeated the incision across Johnson's thigh, stomach, and even across Johnson's forehead. The results were the same. There were also no burn marks or blisters on the sergeant's legs or the bottom of his feet.

At first, the captain didn't believe everything Kapp told him about the ordeal he and his stepbrother had been through.

"It must have been the drug they gave you," stated Captain Carter.

"But it looked like the same drug they gave my stepbrother, and it killed him."

"It couldn't have been. Were both drugs the same color?" Dr. Carter asked.

"Yes, a reddish color," said Kapp.

"And was that the first time they had ever given you and your brother drugs?"

"Yes, of course, the guards could have put something in our food," Kapp stated.

"Hmm," Captain Carter sighed. He placed his hand on his chin.

"No. Since you didn't notice a change in your body before then, the drug you received at the castle had to be the cause. Now, what story will you tell General Patton and the army?"

"I'm going to tell him exactly what I told you," Johnson proclaimed without reservation.

"No, son, I wouldn't advise that. Remember, you're a Negro, and a Negro the white man can't kill would cause hysteria the likes of which we have never seen. The fact that the Nazis invented such a drug and gave it to you wouldn't matter. The only thing that would occupy white folk's minds back home is that a nigger is indestructible. The fear that would cause would be catastrophic for our entire race. It wouldn't be just you; they would believe every Negro soldier had it, and you know what would happen. The extermination of the Jews would be mercy killings compared to the mass butchering that would occur across America of our people, not to mention what they would do to every Colored soldier over here. And they would put you in a hole so deep in the ground not even the Devil would descend to such depths to claim your soul."

"You're right, captain; I hadn't considered it that way. But what should I say? I must tell them something."

Captain Carter reflected for a moment.

"Well, the best lie is a simple one and one that's partially true," the captain said. "There have been reports of Nazi doctors performing gruesome experiments on Jewish prisoners. One Nazi, in particular, Dr. Mengele, is known as the Angel of Death. One report says he took the eyeball of a child from one twin and attached it to the back of the head of the other twin. So you will tell them how you and Private Penson got caught, but they kept the two of you alive for so many months for analysis. They were interested in seeing if Negros reacted differently than white men under certain conditions to prove that the Negro race is inferior. They moved the two of you from place to place for testing. They tested hallucinogenic drugs on Private Penson until one of them finally killed him. But you were given strength and endurance tests. They tested you to see how long you could stand the cold and hold your breath underwater. Don't go into a lot of detail; keep it simple."

"What should I say about how I escaped?" "When it comes to what people will believe,

the most believable explanation is usually the most unlikely. They will think it's so implausible; it must be true."

"Okay," began Johnson, "so I'll tell them that the Nazis burned Private Penson's body last night and then left. Two Jerries buried him on the dirt floor of the dungeon when, suddenly, another Jerry ran in and gave them an order, and all three hurried away and never returned. For hours, I heard nothing. I usually could hear footsteps in the corridor, but everything was quiet and still. No one came to bring food or to check on me. Something had happened. So, I rose and started up the steps, and to my surprise, when I reached the door, it was unlocked. I walked down the corridor and up two more flights of steps, then through a narrow passageway until I suddenly stood in a vast hallway leading to other rooms. No one was in sight. It looked like the Nazis had left in a hurry. There was trash on the floor. Pillows, blankets, and empty cans of food rations were lying around. I checked several rooms off the hallway. They were all empty.

I called out, and all I heard was my voice echoing back. So I returned to the dungeon, retrieved Private Penson's body, and walked out of the castle. I walked through the woods all night for miles. I didn't know where I was or where I was going. I just kept on walking. When morning came, I rested by a big tree in the woods. That's when I heard the shell blasts. So, I got up and walked toward the blasting. Minutes later, I stepped out of the woods into a clearing and stood on a hill where I looked down and saw the battle in progress."

"That sounds good, but it's much too long. Remember, keep it short and simple. Don't make up a lot of details. If they ask for specifics, tell them you don't know or can't remember."

"What will you tell them about your examination of me?"

"That you're alright considering the tests they put you through," said Captain Carter.

"What if they say several soldiers saw me getting shot?"

"Look, there's no evidence anywhere on your body that you got shot. So, no matter what anybody says, you couldn't have been shot, and that's that. No one is going to believe that you were peppered with bullets, and the bullets didn't penetrate your body. The shell blasts filled the ravine with smoke. So, my answer will be that the smoke must have impaired the vision of some of the soldiers. Don't worry. No one will contradict it because everyone will see that you're not wounded. So, what other explanation could there be? Do you think any soldiers will risk being called crazy for seeing things? By this time tomorrow, no one will be talking about how many times they saw you get shot."

"That sounds reasonable. Except for the bullet holes in my pants, said Johnson."

"Not after I shred and burn them."

"Burn them? Won't that draw attention?"

"Well, then, I'll bury them." Sergeant Johnson stepped off the examination table and walked over to a corner of the tent where he had placed his burnt and bullet-riddled green trousers.

"Here you go, Captain," said Johnson as he handed the pants to Carter. Captain Carter held them up. There were at least twelve bullet holes in the front and back. Carter shook his head in amazement, then stuffed the pants into his medical bag.

"After I dispose of these, I'll return and escort you to General Patton. He's expecting you at 1600 hours." Captain Carter checked his watch.

"You've got about twenty-five minutes to get dressed."

After Captain Carter left, Kapp quickly donned a fresh uniform. He checked his appearance in the small handheld mirror on the foldable wooden desk. Kapp looked no different than before his capture except for a haircut and shave. He rubbed his right hand across his mouth, cheeks, and cleft chin. His cinnamon complexion was smooth and without blemish except for the small diamond-shaped birthmark on the bridge of his nose. Females had always found Kapp attractive, especially his root beer-colored eyes. His wife Clare was the only girl who hadn't been so enamored with his looks, at least not at first. That was because she was the most beautiful girl at Morris Brown, with a slew of suitors chasing her.

Kapp smiled, thinking about seeing his wife again. For the first time since he entered the war, he was sure he was going home. Captain Carter entered as he placed the mirror back on the desk.

"It's time," said the captain.

Kapp grabbed his cap off the table and headed out of the tent.

Captain Carter stopped him. He checked Kapp's appearance one last time. After looking the sergeant over, the captain placed his right hand on Kapp's shoulder.

"Bring us home, son."

CHAPTER TWENTY-TWO

Thy soul shall find itself alone
'Mid dark thoughts of the gray tombstone.

Edgar Allen Poe

Sunset, May 1, 1945
Basel, Switzerland

Otto could feel the serum racing through his bloodstream. The Elixir of Life's absorption into his body was quick and complete, taking effect only seconds after Dr. Weiss injected it into his arm. He pictured the serum moving through his veins like a current of rushing water through a canal. Otto immediately felt lightheaded and off-balance, with symptoms of vertigo. He lifted his feet onto the black wooden stool in front of him.

Otto didn't want to be put to sleep first. He didn't trust the doctor and wanted to be conscious and aware of what was happening. Instead, Dr. Weiss doped him with a mild tranquilizer.

Leaning back in the black leather chair, he gazed out of the open window in one of the three bedrooms in the doctor's cottage. A cool breeze blew in. It was sundown. Vibrant colors of yellow, orange, and red streaks brushed the sky.

Burning from the serum started in his toes first and swiftly moved up his body to his legs until it reached his thighs. It then traveled to his stomach, chest, neck, and head. His blood felt like it was on fire. The worst burning was in his groin.

He had to be strong, he thought. He had to take the pain no matter how excruciating it felt. He had to die before he could live. The pain would be worth it in the end. He would have endless life and would never have to face permanent death again.

As the burning grew more intense, Otto couldn't keep still. He twisted and turned his body while grinding his teeth. Otto banged his fists on the arms of the chair. He could feel himself dying and was afraid. Suddenly, the face of the young Negro soldier screaming flashed in Otto's mind, and panic washed over him. He bled thoughts of doubt.

What if he had selected the wrong vial? What if he wasn't dying to live but simply dying? He carefully examined both the flasks Dr. Weiss injected into Arnulf and Dag. He viewed them in the sunlight for color determination. At the doctor's suggestion, Otto even turned the vials upside down several times to see how the serum flowed. He then held the tubes in the palm of his hand, trying to determine their weight.

"Take your time," said Dr. Weiss.

Otto examined each vial for over ten minutes. When it was time to select the vial for his injection, he Otto took just as long to choose. Dr. Weiss congratulated him on selecting correctly, but what if the doctor lied? It is possible. Dr. Weiss never hid his objections to Otto taking the serum. The doctor didn't think him worthy.

Otto thought, *maybe the doctor switched the serum before injecting it into my arm.*

Otto screamed. "Mein Got! Mein Got! Help me! Mein Got!"

In agony, Otto screamed for an hour then suddenly stopped.

On May 1, 1945, at approximately 7:46 PM, Nazi Colonel Otto Victor Strauss, age 25, of Klagenfurt, Austria, died.

CHAPTER TWENTY-THREE

There is one thing you men will be able to say
when you go home.
You may all thank God that thirty years
from now when you are sitting with your
grandson on your knee, and he asks,
"Grandfather, what did you do in World War II?"
You won't have to say, "I shoveled manure in
Mississippi."

General George S. Patton

Noon, May 5, 1945
Steyr, Austria

Finally, the war was over. The news was that
Admiral Hans-Georg von Friedeburg, Commander-
in-Chief of the German Navy, met with General
Eisenhower at the general's headquarters in Reins,
France. They negotiated the official truce just as the
Third Army and the 761st Tank Battalion rolled into
Steyr, Austria, to meet the Russians.

The Black soldiers of the 761st had spent one
hundred and eighty days on the front lines and had
fought and defeated the best of Hitler's Wehrmacht.

News of the war's end swept through the camp with shouts of joy and tears of relief.

It was all over. Every soldier thanked God they had survived. Soon, they would all board a ship headed for home. But no one was going home just yet. There was now a post-war occupation to manage. The 71st Infantry Division had to negotiate the surrender of one hundred thousand German soldiers who didn't want to be taken by the Russians, fearing mistreatment.

It was a sunny day. The sky was a deep velvet blue dotted with puffs of fluffy, white clouds. The 761st lined up their tanks along a small bridge and stood in front of their Shermans, waiting for the surrender ceremonies to begin. Sergeant Johnson stood in front of the last tank in the column, coming off the bridge with a bright new shining Silver Star pinned to his dress green army jacket. He was awarded the medal two days ago for his actions during the fighting in the ravine.

To his right was Private First Class Ray Wilson, a pushy, dark-skinned twenty-year-old from Detroit with a reputation for being a smart mouth and getting into everybody's business. Kapp glanced down the line. Captain Carter was standing near the start of the column. The captain had been right. All the talk about how often he had gotten shot stopped once the word got out that he wasn't even wounded. Most of the discussion about his heroics waned over the past several days with the anticipation of the war's end. No one wanted to talk about fighting now. There were far better things for everyone to talk about, like going home and seeing their wives, children, parents, and friends.

Kapp was still looking down the line when a jeep waving a blue flag with a white star in the center drove toward the bridge. Standing in the jeep, straight and tall like an ivory statue, was General George Smith Patton. He wore his four-star helmet, white riding britches, and high-polished black riding boots. His gun holster was strapped to the general's waist, carrying his two pistols with the pearl handle.

Kapp and all the Black troops of the 761st snapped to attention and saluted. General Patton gave a sharp salute as he drove across the bridge. But as Patton passed Kapp, the general suddenly flashed him a look. It wasn't the stern, proud gaze the general usually gave but a suspicious glare. It sent a shiver down Kapp's spine that even Private Wilson noticed. "What's wrong, Sarge? You all right? You look kinda shaky."

"I'm fine," said Kapp, irritated that the private had seen his body shake like a man shivering in the cold.

"Oh, I just thought that one of those bullets that missed you finally caught up with ya," Wilson replied with a smirk on his face.

Kapp's face turned red. "It did, but I countered it with this," Kapp stated while slowly rotating his tightly balled fist in the air.

"AT-TEN-TION!"

Kapp and Wilson immediately faced Captain Carter, straightened their shoulders, and saluted. The captain tilted his head toward Wilson.

"You're dismissed, private."

"Yes, sir." Private Wilson departed.

"What was that all about?" the captain asked.

Kapp shook his head. "Nothing, he was just running his mouth, and I guess I let it get to me."

"Look, Johnson." Captain Carter grabbed Kapp by the arm and led the sergeant away.

"You're going to have to be careful and not bring attention to yourself in any way until you get stateside. Thankfully, that won't be long because Colonel Baker has signed the papers for you to be sent home with an honorable discharge, effective immediately." "Why am I going home so soon before everyone else?" Kapp asked.

"Two reasons," Captain Carter explained. "First, your capture by the Germans makes you a prisoner of war, and with the status of POW on your record, it puts you first in line to ship out along with the wounded. Second, and more importantly, the army doesn't want any questions from the Negro press about experiments the Nazis allegedly performed on you and Private Penson. Terrible things happen in war. Millions of people have suffered horribly in this one. You're one of them. The army's view is that your story isn't any more tragic than anyone else's. So, pack up. You leave tomorrow at 0700 hours for France, where you will get on board the USS Enterprise for New York. And the sooner you leave, the better off we'll all be. Your stepbrother's body will be on the same ship." Captain Carter patted Kapp on the back and left.

Kapp walked back to his tent to lay down. He didn't bother gathering his things. Kapp had nothing to pack. No doubt, the army shipped his personal belongings home after he and Pauli disappeared. German soldiers were ordered to kill and not capture Negro troops. That the two of them were dead was the logical assumption.

For the first time, Kapp thought about how Clare must have cried after reading the army's standard "I Regret to Inform You" letter and how she would be that much happier when she sees him now. He smiled at the thought and closed his eyes. He could see his wife's small oval-shaped face and slender body in his mind's eye. He took a deep breath, imagining he was inhaling the scent of her jasmine perfume. For the first time in months, he felt calm and relaxed.

It had been a long time since he slept in a bed. Though the cot was narrow and lumpy in places, it felt good. The only noise came from the muffled voices of soldiers laughing and talking outside his tent. Kapp thought he heard his name spoken for a second and lifted his head slightly off his pillow to hear. But drowsiness quickly overtook him, and within seconds, the image of Clare and the sound of voices faded away.

CHAPTER TWENTY-FOUR

"Praise be to God!
The diabolical work of the Lebensborn has at
last been destroyed."

Cardinal Faulhaber Speaking
in Munich, Spring 1945

Noon, May 5, 1945
Basel, Switzerland

"What about the Oberstfuhrer?" Arnulf asked.

"He has yet to awaken?"

Both he and Dag were wearing civilian clothes: Arnulf in dark blue, khaki pants and a light blue long-sleeved shirt and Dag in black trousers and a white T-shirt. The two woke from death yesterday at approximately seven o'clock in the morning, while Hans had awakened the day before.

"Leave him where he is. He has a slow metabolism, so it's taking longer for the serum to revive the Kommandant," grunted Dr. Weiss in a weak, raspy voice. He lay in bed, Hans on one side of him clutching his hand, and Dag and Arnulf standing on the opposite side looking on.

The boy, Adok, was sitting on the floor with his legs crossed in front of the window, playing with a spinning top. The room was dim, with only sparse sunlight seeping through the drawn curtains.

"I'm dying," Dr. Weiss blurted out painfully. "I have only hours left now."

The doctor's skin was chalky-white and thin, thin enough that the veins in his face were visible.

"What shall we do? Where shall we go?" asked Dag.

"Go back to your families, what's left of them, and live your lives. When the Kommandant rises, he'll come for you, and I'm sure he'll find you, however long it takes. There are 5,000 marks in the envelopes in the drawer for each of you. Take the money and leave. Hans will take care of the boy and me. Take the train to Frankfurt at the Gare Centrale railway station on 10 Gare de Mulhouse Street. But don't drive the military jeep to the station. Ditch it in the woods somewhere along the road before you reach the city. You will have to walk the rest of the way. Otherwise, you will attract attention and may get arrested. Being a Nazi is no longer advantageous now that the war is over. Now go!"

As Arnulf and Dag were leaving, Dr. Weiss looked at Hans.

"What about me, uncle?" asked Hans in a firm but sad voice.

Hearing his nephew speak was like hearing the voice of his twin brother Johann. Dr. Weiss felt proud of himself for having saved Hans from the Flossenburg concentration camp. Even prouder for inventing the serum that gave his nephew back his voice and restored his brain function. Hans stood before him, a new man. He was a handsome boy. Hans was five feet and eleven inches, much taller than he and his father. But he had Johann's kind ways and gentle nature. He treated Dr. Weiss with all the affection of an adoring son to a beloved father, which Weiss knew he didn't deserve.

"When I die, bury me in the woods behind the shed next to my wife, Gitta's grave. Then take Adok back to his parents in Slupsk, Poland."

"You will find the child's address in the suitcase under the bed, along with my Will and further instructions. Once you reunite Adok with his parents, I want you to leave the country. Go as far away as you can, to…" Weiss paused. "…to Canada. Get married and have children, lots of sons preferably, and I pray they'll be just like their father--God-fearing and kind. They will need to counteract the evil that will come about once Kommandant Strauss rises and builds his army of immortals. Besides the seven vials of serum in my alabaster case, I have hidden four pints of the elixir along with the formula in the shed behind some planks in the wall. I leave it all to the Kommandant as promised. Put them in his room so he will have them when he finally wakes up.

The world doesn't know what it's in for. But I don't regret what I've done. I am a scientist and a doctor. Those in my profession invent to prolong life, and I've done just that. If the world judges me, let it be for my creation alone, not how men use it. Thousands of people are killed in vehicular accidents every year, but that doesn't mean Henry Ford shouldn't have invented the automobile. All of mankind's inventions are advances in man's evolution, the serum more so than any other," he sighed.

Dr. Weiss groaned and gripped his nephew's hand to endure an intense attack of searing pain. Grinding his teeth, the doctor leaned slightly forward and bore down against his nephew. He felt drained once the pain subsided and could sense death was imminent.

Don't fight it. It will only prolong the process and intensify the pain intervals. Just let go.

The doctor obeyed the voice inside his head, drew in one long, deep breath, and slowly let it out. Calmness immediately washed over him. The pain was gone. He lay still and listened to the rotating sound of Adok's spinning top twirling around and around on the end table beside his bed until his hearing slowly faded.

Dr. Weiss looked around the room at the cream-plastered walls and wood-planked ceiling. He glanced at the two lamps with shades of a red-rose tapestry that his wife Gitta purchased, then at their wedding picture on top of the dresser. His gaze finally rested on Hans again, who was now kneeling beside him, quietly sobbing. The tears in his nephew's big green eyes sparkled as they rolled down the boy's ruddy face. Mustering up all his strength, Dr. Weiss lifted his right hand and touched his nephew's wet cheek with his trembling fingers. He was glad Hans was here.

It was comforting to know that someone in his life still cared for him and would miss him when he was gone.

Suddenly, the doctor's hand slipped from his nephew's face. The room was now a blur of faint, indistinguishable shadows. The doctor drew in one loud, gasping breath as his eyelids closed. And that is how the infamous Dr. Josef Wilhelm Weiss, the genius physician and the inventor of the Elixir of Life, died, like most humans die--unknown to the world.

CHAPTER TWENTY-FIVE

We have to dare to be ourselves,
however frightening or strange
that self may prove to be.

May Sarton

Hans wiped the tears from his eyes, walked over to the table, and stared at the serum, remembering his uncle's words: "Besides the eight vials in my alabaster case, I have hidden four pints of the elixir along with the formula in the shed behind some planks in the wall. I leave everything to the Kommandant as promised. Put them in his room so he will have them when he wakes up."

Hans looked over at his dead uncle's face, then again at the vials, and shook his head. *"Some promises should never be made and never be kept,"* said the voice inside his head. One-by-one, he took the vials and smashed each against the wall in his uncle's bedroom while Adok sat and watched.

"Here," said Hans, extending his hand to Adok. It was the last vial. Adok hopped up, rushed over, took the serum, and threw it against the wall.

"Come, we must bury my uncle." Hans wrapped his uncle up in a bedsheet, lifted the body onto his shoulder and carried him downstairs and outside to the back of the shed.

"There should be a shovel in there."

Adok ran inside and got it. Hans could see Adok was eager to help, so he let the boy dig the grave. When the task became too much for Adok, he took over.

Two hours later, his uncle lay in the ground. Hans stared down at the mound of dirt. His eyes were dry. He had cried as much as he would cry for his uncle. His tears were more for his father, anyway. His father and uncle looked so much alike that Hans imagined it was his father lying there on his deathbed. Hans hadn't known his Uncle Josef that well. He hardly saw him growing up. But Hans sensed that, even as a child, Uncle Josef didn't like his father much. He remembered the night his father came to his uncle for help and how his uncle turned him away.

Had Uncle Josef given my father the money to leave, how much different would my life be now? My parents would still be alive, and I would never have been in Flossenburg, Hans thought.

Hans still believed God existed, but he had changed. He had lost his Christianity somehow. The feeling scared him because he didn't know if he wanted it back.

Hans felt Adok grab hold of his hand. He glanced down at the boy smiling at him.

"I guess I should say a prayer," said Hans. He watched Adok bow his head. He did the same. There was a prolonged moment of silence before Hans finally spoke.

"Rest in peace, Uncle Josef."

Hans turned abruptly and walked into the shed. He lifted the trap door and walked down the steps to his uncle's laboratory. There, he found the hidden serum vials and the formula where his uncle said he had hidden them.

The world is finally rid of one evil man. There is no way I will facilitate the rise of another.

Hans smashed the four pints of elixir on the floor, turned on all the Bunsen burners, and burned the formula.

"Burn all the loose papers you find," he told Adok. Adok obeyed. When done, Hans set fire to the books on the bookshelf, and the two left. They stood outside and watched the shed burn to the ground until the flames died out.

"Are we leaving now?"

"Not yet; there is one more thing we must do. We must hurry before it gets dark," said Hans. They ran back to the cottage. There was a coil of barbed wire in the utility room that his uncle used to fence his vegetable garden. He grabbed it and rushed upstairs. Slowly, he opened the door to the Kommandant's bedroom and went inside. Adok followed. The Kommandant's body was facing the window and slumped in a high-back black leather chair. Quietly, Hans approached. He could hear his heart pounding rapidly in his ears.

What if he revives? Then hurry up!

Hans quickly wrapped the barbed wire around the chair and the colonel's entire body, from his head to his feet, until the Kommandant looked like silver, wired-wrapped mummy. The barbed wire was 18 feet long, enabling Hans to take the end of the cable and thread it through the bedroom door keyhole. Hans then locked the door and pulled the barbed wire as far as it would go down the stairs. He tied the cord around one of the two wooden posts dividing the living room from the dining room. When he was done, he looked at his handy work and then at Adok. Adok looked up at him. Immediately, they both laughed.

"I guess we can go now," said Hans.

Bolting out the door and across the meadow, Adok headed down the dirt road. Hans flung his uncle's black leather satchel across his shoulder and followed. A reddish-orange sunset colored the sky, complemented by a warm, caressing breeze. The town of Basel was eleven miles away. When they reached the city, it was nighttime. The two ran and walked and walked and ran until they saw the pointed rooftops of buildings from a hill.

On the banks of the Rhine, the streets of Basel sparkled with dancing lights reflecting off the water. Hans and Adok raced down the hill onto Market Square, where shops and cafes housed in ancient buildings influenced by Gothic and Renaissance architecture lined brick pavements.

Now that the war was over, there was no fear of bombing. People crammed into the square to shop and celebrate. Switzerland was a neutral country and didn't participate in the war. Still, several Swiss cities, including Basel, were mistakenly bombed by Allied Forces intended for other targets.

Hans led the way as he and Adok weaved through the crowds. Hans felt Adok grab hold of his arm. Adok's grip was tight. He was holding onto Hans with both hands. Hans stopped and bent down in front of Adok.

"Hop on."

Adok obeyed. He continued with Adok on his back. He crossed over to the other side of the street and entered the oldest café in Basel. Confiserie Schiesser, opened in 1870, was famous for its candied oranges and homemade ice cream.

"What flavor of ice cream would you like?" asked Hans as Adok slid off his back.

The café owner named the flavors: "Schokolade, Vanille oder Erdbeere?"

Hans noticed a frown form on Adok's face. The boy shook his head rapidly from side to side.

"No chocolate! I hate chocolate!" Tears filled Adok's eyes. "No chocolate!"

Everyone in the café turned and looked. Hans put his arm around Adok as Adok buried his face in Hans' shirt.

"Some other time," said Hans, picking up Adok. He carried Adok across the Middle Bridge and checked into the Les Trois Rois Grand Hotel.

"Tomorrow, I'll register my uncle's Will in court, and we'll travel to Slupsk," he told Adok as he followed the bellhop to their room, still holding Adok in his arms.

Hans woke up before daybreak the following day and walked out onto the balcony. Adok was still asleep. Hans hardly slept. Too many thoughts and images of Flossenburg haunted his dreams. Oddly, he had no problems sleeping in the labor camp. Sleep was a welcome escape from the horrible reality he faced when awake. He always prayed before he lay down. Not anymore. Not that he didn't desire to talk to God; he couldn't pray to God. It was as if his mind blocked any thoughts of the Almighty from entering. Now, to him, God was just a hollow three-letter word. He didn't know how this could be possible after all he suffered. He never once doubted that his faith sustained him during those terrible years. The belief that seemed so strong months ago seemed lost to him now. Hans wondered if the serum was the cause. He hadn't destroyed all his uncle's papers. His uncle had documented the serum's effects on the body and how a person would feel after being resurrected. Those notes he kept, and some others. So far, the documentation was accurate, but there was no way his uncle could know all the effects.

Hans woke from death two days ago, full of strength and surging with energy. The scars, bruises, and cuts left on his body from the beatings had disappeared. He opened his mouth for the first time in over a year, and words, not grunts, came out. He wasn't born with a mental deficiency. The Elixir of Life, therefore, restored his brain function. But Hans felt his mind was different. As damaged as his brain had been, his awareness of God remained intact during his time in prison. He sensed God was there during those dark days, guiding and protecting him. Now, that sense was gone.

Where did it go? He asked himself. There was no reply.

Hans went to answer the knock on the door. Two bellhops entered. One rolled in a table with breakfast. The other carried a garment rack with clothes Hans ordered last night from the men's store next to the hotel.

"Were you able to find clothes to fit the boy?"

"Yes, sir," answered the attendant. "The store manager selected several things for the two of you that he hopes you will like. If not, we will be happy to bring you some other selections. Would you like to see them now, sir?"

"No, I'll look at them later. Just hang the clothes in the closet."

"Yes, sir."

Hans retrieved money from his uncle's satchel and handed it to the two bellhops.

"Thank you, sir. Will there be anything else, sir," said the last bellhop before leaving.

Hans shook his head.

I'm the same age as you, and I'm hardly a sir. But I guess with money comes clout.

Hans inherited a hefty sum from his uncle and was grateful for that. Most of it came from his uncle's second wife, who's wealthy father built cargo ships and fishing boats for a living. Hans was going to Canada, a multi-millionaire. It didn't make up for his parents' death or his ordeal at Flossenburg, but it did guarantee a more comfortable life ahead.

Hans looked at the clock on the nightstand beside the bed and woke Adok. They had two hours before he had to be at the magistrate's office at seven o'clock to register the Will. Hans then went to the bank to sign documents to transfer his uncle's estate into his name and to have money available when Hans arrived in Vancouver. He had to do this before 3:00 PM to catch the railway to Germany.

Hans and Adok had to take a train to Berlin and then a bus to Slupsk to travel from Switzerland to Poland. They arrived in Berlin before sundown. Berlin was in ruins. In every direction, bombed buildings were as far as the eye could see. Piles of bricks, crushed glass, bits and pieces of furniture, and other debris cluttered the streets. The Allied Forces of France, Britain, America, and the Soviet Union occupied the city. Each country had designated areas they claimed as their territory. Security was tight. No one could enter or leave without being checked.

Hans was also grateful for his uncle's planning. Uncle Josef had thought of everything before his death and had official travel passports made for the two, listing Switzerland as their birthplace. If questioned, Hans was to say they were traveling to Poland to visit relatives. Fortunately, the train stopped in the U.S. Zone. Despite the hours of waiting in long lines, they breezed through the checkpoints with no hassle and walked three blocks to the bus station to catch the last departure to Poland.

They arrived in Slupsk at four o'clock in the morning. The streets were dark and deserted. All the passengers got off the bus and walked directly to the hotel and restaurant across from the bus stop. Hans was about to enter, too, but Adok wouldn't go. Hans couldn't blame the boy's eagerness to see his parents. "Which way," said Hans. He followed Adok down four blocks before turning the corner and continuing eight more blocks. They came to an area well-lit by streetlamps. It was a park two blocks long. Hans watched as Adok stood under a streetlight and stared at a tall evergreen before walking away. He followed Adok around the block and passed a sign that read Jezey Waldorf's Park before they crossed the street again.

They continued down a very narrow block. Adok stopped again. This time, Adok stood in front of a store with the windows boarded up and a broken shingle hanging on one hinge that read, "Makowski'sBrutc."

Suddenly, Adok ran. Hans ran after him to the end of the block, through a patch of grass lined with trees, and across a small bridge overlooking a narrow river. Hans continued to follow Adok another two blocks before Adok ran up the steps of a house. A lamp post stood directly in front of the residence. The door of the house was off its hinges.

When Hans reached the door, Adok was already inside, running through each room, screaming his parents and baby brother's name. The light from the streetlight cast shadows on the walls. The house was ransacked. Overturned and broken furniture cluttered every room. Adok kept calling his mother and father, but no one answered.

Finally, Adok stopped running. Hans could hear him crying and followed the sobbing to a room in the back of the house. He found Adok sitting on the floor against a wall with his legs against his chest and his head buried between his knees. Against the opposite wall were two beds. One was a small single bed, the other a baby bed. Hans sat down beside Adok. The curtains were torn down, letting the moonlight stream through the window. Hans wrapped his arms around Adok, and the two huddled together until morning.

Morning came quickly. Both he and Adok had fallen asleep. The sound of footsteps creeping slowly along the corridor woke Hans up. The squeaking noise stopped at the bedroom door. Hans could hear breathing. Before he could stand up, the door flung open, and the person was in the room.

"Who are you, and what are you doing here?" asked a short, chubby middle-aged man. He held a pistol in his hand. He was wearing a beige shirt and dark brown pants.

Hans was about to answer when the old man recognized Adok. Adok was waking up, yawning and rubbing his eyes.

"Adok! Adok!" the man repeated. "My boy, is that you?"

Adok focused his eyes on the man, then jumped up and rushed into the man's arms.

"Mr. Polanski," Adok shouted. They hugged each other.

"I'm so glad to see you, my boy," he said.

"Where are my parents?"

Hans pressed his back against the wall to brace himself for bad news.

Mr. Polanski shook his head.

"When you went missing, your parents searched for you. Everyone here in the neighborhood did, and so did the local Polish police--block after block, for miles we searched. When they couldn't find you, your parents visited the German Consulate. There were rumors of Germans kidnapping Polish children and adopting them as their own. Your parents believed that was what happened to you. Of course, the consulate denied it. Since there was no proof, nothing was done, either by the German or Polish authorities. But your father wouldn't let it go. Your father used to believe in Hitler. Now, he was angry. He began to speak out against the Nazi Regime and became a part of the Polish underground resistance movement. A group of twenty would sneak over into Germany and sabotage their ammunition supplies. Then, one morning, the SS stormed into the house and dragged your parents out, little Arie too, and shot them all right out in the street. The SS banged on all the doors and woke up the entire neighborhood so everyone could witness it."

Hans thought Adok would cry. He didn't. Adok remained silent.

When Mr. Polanski finished, Adok merely turned and looked up at him.

The look in the boy's eyes was one of sadness but resilience. Hans knew what it meant. He didn't give Adok a verbal reply. He merely nodded. Hans had always wanted a younger brother. Adok would do.

CHAPTER TWENTY-SIX

The same sun that rises over castles and welcomes
the day spills over buildings into the
streets where orphans play, and only you
can see the good in broken things you took
my heart of stone and made it home and set this
prisoner free.

Bethany Dillon

Morning, May 19, 1945
New York, New York

As the USS Enterprise slowly maneuvered into New York's harbor, a crowd of exuberant soldiers stood on the deck, shouting and waving down at the large group of family, friends, and well-wishers lined the docks, cheering their arrival.

Kapp was also on deck. But instead of looking ahead of him, he was standing by himself on the opposite side of the ship, staring out at the vast ocean, as if he had left something behind, was searching the waves to find it.

He was finally home. But he didn't feel happy or sad about it. He longed to see his wife, Clare, and his mother and stepfather again. Still, he felt confused and conflicted.

He was home from the war with a different body, not one ravished and broken like so many other wounded soldiers that would have been normal. Instead, he had a body he didn't know, that wasn't his own, a body that did extraordinary things he was afraid to talk about and couldn't comprehend. The person or persons responsible for his altered new self were somewhere in Germany. He was seeking answers.

Unfortunately, now that he was back in America, all the burning questions that plagued him would never be satisfied. He wanted to know what to expect if the abilities he now possessed were permanent or only temporary. If bullets and fire couldn't kill him, what could? Would he still be able to have children? Would his children also inherit his abilities? There were so many questions, and there was no one he could turn to for the answers. He felt lost and alone.

Kapp reached into his pants pocket and pulled out the address and phone number of Captain Carter's residence in New York. "If you ever need to talk," the captain told him. Kapp considered staying in New York until the captain returned from the war. He felt a desire to be around the only person who knew of his condition. Kapp wasn't even sure he should return to his family. They still thought he was dead. Kapp hadn't written them, so maybe it would be best if they just went on believing he had been killed in action. Thoughts about what would happen if he returned home worried him. He couldn't keep his secret forever, even if he tried to. A man and woman can't live together for years and not discover something they don't want the other to know. Eventually, he would have to tell Clare. How would she take it? What would she think of him? The possibility of losing her love was too unbearable to contemplate.

The more Kapp thought about it, the more resolute he became. He was never going home. He would make a new life for himself here in New York. The decision immediately put Kapp's mind at ease, even as it broke his heart. So, he focused instead on the seagulls circling the sky and diving into the water to scoop up fish. One-by-one, they dived in like jet-propelled rockets.

"Kapp."

Kapp was startled at suddenly hearing a soft, soprano voice. It sounded like…Kapp turned around, and there stood Clare.

"Surprise," she said, smiling. She wore a black dress with a V-neckline trimmed in white and a big white bow in the center. Her silky black hair was parted down the middle and rolled in a big curl on both sides. People often said Clare looked like Lena Horne. Kapp always thought she looked more like Dorothy Dandridge. Whichever film star she resembled, she was beautiful. He had forgotten just how lovely. Kapp quickly pulled his wife into his arms and planted a long, passionate kiss on her ruby-red lips.

"What are you doing here? How did you know I was coming home?"

"What are you doing here? How did you know I was coming home?"

"I received a letter from a doctor in your battalion, Captain Robert Carter. It arrived three days ago, explaining that the army had made a mistake. Captain Carter stated that you escaped from the Germans. He told me about Pauli and about…"

Kapp looked into his wife's eyes and knew she knew everything.

"Whatever happened," she whispered, gazing up at him. "Whatever they did to you, and however you have changed, it's all right, darling. We will face it together. I love you, and it's going to be all right."

Overcome with emotion, Kapp pressed his face against his wife's cheek. He held Clare close, close enough to hear both their heartbeats. His decision not to return home now seemed foolish and insane.

"Come on, babe," Kapp said, suddenly eager to leave. He locked arms with his wife. But before Kapp walked away, he felt an impulse to turn and gaze at the ocean one last time. Kapp knew his life was forever linked to Germany and that someday, he would have to return. What the future held; he didn't know. But for now, he was happy the war was over and relieved he was going home.

AFTERWORD

MAY 19, 1945
Somewhere on the Atlantic Ocean

When Hans Johann Weiss and Adok Bohdan Makowski boarded the ship to Canada, no one would have guessed them to be victims of the Nazi Regime. They looked to be the offspring of wealthy, influential parents who had never known a day's hardship or given a reason to worry. Hans wore a dark blue, double-breasted, pin-striped suit with a white silk shirt, square cuff links of blue sapphire, a red silk tie, and black, high-polished shoes. His attire made a striking contrast to his slicked-back, wavy red hair and green eyes. Adok wore white pants, a short, navy blue, sea captain's jacket, and a blue and white pin-striped shirt with an open-fly collar. His ringlets of thick blonde curls crowned the top of his head.

They traveled first class and never left each other's side. Three days ago, the two set sail from London.

It was a bright Sunday morning. The two stood on the deck, looking out at sea. Hans leaned over the rail as if he was listening to the sound of waves splashing against the side of the ship, while Adok gazed up at the sky and then upon the vast expanse of the sea. Every passenger who walked by noticed them and wondered who they were and what held their attention. One six-year-old boy ran up beside Adok and asked.

"What you staring at?"

"Seagulls."

"What seagulls?"

"The ones diving into the water and scooping up fish," said Adok.

"I don't see any seagulls," said the six-year-old.

"Come on, Frederick, and leave those two young men alone," said the boy's mother.

Hans and Adok didn't even bother to look back as his mother dragged him away. Their gaze was locked on the distant horizon of the Atlantic, stretching thousands of miles away.

"A woman has come to meet him," said Adok. "She's pretty."

"Yes, I know. It's his wife," said Hans. "She's telling him that Captain Carter wrote and told her about the serum and that everything's going to be all right," said Hans.

"They're walking away now," said Adok. "No, wait. He's stopping and turning in this direction. He's looking straight at us. Do you think he can see us like we can see and hear him?"

"I don't know," said Hans. "But I have a feeling that one day, whether we want to or not, we're going to find out."

To be Continued…

www.ingramcontent.com/pod-product-compliance
Lightning Source LLC
Chambersburg PA
CBHW032033310726
48972CB00002B/657